"Intricate and complex, both reportage and confession, littered with moments of meaning—or at least a meaningful search for same…An elegant portrait of a man half-fractured, half-intact—a post-war somebody caught between repair and capitulation, controlling his own fate and imprisoned by regret."
— *Texas Observer*

"In the layered narratives of Baxter's piercing first novel, a young American returned from Iraq struggles to find a new life in Europe."
— *New York Times Book Review* (Editor's Choice)

"[A] quietly powerful novel…Baxter's clean and direct prose generates its own momentum. He chooses not to create a tidy drama where characters are explained by their pasts. Rather, he creates something bigger and more true…Baxter has written a big book in a lean one, and he has written a book where everything is happening while at the same time nothing is happening. Put another way, the book succeeds."   — Daily Beast

"Absorbing, atmospheric, and enigmatic…With its disorienting juxtaposition of the absolutely ordinary and the strange and vaguely threatening, the novel evokes the work of Franz Kafka and Haruki Murakami, while its oblique explorations of memory suggest a debt to W. G. Sebald…Baxter's provocative, unsettling novel is, among other things, about the inexorability of identity and 'the immortality of violence.'"
— *Los Angeles Times*

"THE APARTMENT succeeds as a novel of intense intro-
spection."   —*Boston Globe*

"[A] lucidly written and astutely observed debut
novel…Despite the lack of incident, the novel exerts a hypnotic force…It is precisely this sort of subversion, along
with the author's shimmering prose, that makes THE
APARTMENT such a surprisingly compelling read and so
apropos; it captures the mood of the current moment and
what seems to be a new 'lost generation,' one formed not
so much by exposure to violence, as immunity to and alienation from it. Once upon a time, there was no place like
home; in Mr. Baxter's world, home, it seems, is no place."
                                             —*New York Times*

"THE APARTMENT impressively and tactfully covers everything from the effects of American interventionism on
its relationship with Europe to questions of personal identity."   —*Esquire*

"'I was born to hate the place I came from.' Greg Baxter's
THE APARTMENT is a short but powerful exploration of
that sentiment, uttered halfway through the novel by its narrator, a 41-year-old American ex-Navy officer and Iraq War
veteran."   —*Chicago Tribune*

"A formally and thematically ambitious debut novel that
aims very high and rarely falls short…This shows both a

mastery of literary technique and a refusal to see such technique as an end in itself…A very smart novel that recognizes the limits of intelligence and the distortions of memory."   —*Kirkus Reviews* (starred review)

"Baxter's thoughtful, quietly penetrating book is for those seeking more than a quick read."   —*Library Journal*

"A true gem…lucid, often hypnotic, and, at times, even transporting…[He] keeps his sentences short, his adjectives limited, his pacing leisurely…Baxter has the makings of a talented novelist."

—*Los Angeles Review of Books*

"Where the novel shines most is in the telling—the slow, deliberate narrative unfolds like a quiet symphony, and Baxter's prose lingers inexplicably, like a beautifully sad song."

—*Publishers Weekly*

The Apartment

The Apartment

A Novel

GREG BAXTER

TWELVE

New York   Boston

Copyright © 2012 by Greg Baxter
Reading Group Guide copyright © 2014 by Hachette Book Group, Inc.
All rights reserved. In accordance with the U.S. Copyright Act of 1976, the scanning, uploading, and electronic sharing of any part of this book without the permission of the publisher constitutes unlawful piracy and theft of the author's intellectual property. If you would like to use material from the book (other than for review purposes), prior written permission must be obtained by contacting the publisher at permissions@hbgusa.com. Thank you for your support of the author's rights.

Twelve
Hachette Book Group
1290 Avenue of the Americas
New York, NY 10104

www.HachetteBookGroup.com

Printed in the United States of America

RRD-C

First Grand Central Publishing hardcover edition: December 2013
First trade edition: November 2014
10 9 8 7 6 5 4 3 2 1

Twelve is an imprint of Grand Central Publishing.
The Twelve name and logo are trademarks of Hachette Book Group, Inc.

The Hachette Speakers Bureau provides a wide range of authors for speaking events. To find out more, go to www.hachettespeakersbureau.com or call (866) 376-6591.

The publisher is not responsible for websites (or their content) that are not owned by the publisher.

Library of Congress Cataloging-in-Publication Data
  The apartment : a novel / Greg Baxter. — First Grand Central Publishing Edition.
    pages cm
  ISBN 978-1-4555-7478-0 (hardback) — ISBN 978-1-4789-2451-7 (audio download) — ISBN 978-1-4555-4771-5 (ebook)
1. Apartment dwellers — Europe — Fiction. 2. Authorship — Fiction. 3. War — Fiction. 4. City and town life — Europe — Fiction. I. Title.
  PS36-2.A977A63 2013
  813'.6 — dc23
                        2013017807

ISBN 978-1-4555-4836-1 (pbk.)

For BH

The Apartment

IT'S THE MIDDLE OF DECEMBER, and everything is frozen over. I arrived six weeks ago with an old, worn-out pair of brown leather shoes. One night I walked around the city with a girl I'd met, and the next day I bought myself some lined, warm, waterproof boots. I threw the brown shoes away. I would have kept them for the spring, but I ruined them by heating them on the radiator at night.

I'm from the desert—a town with a small population. When I was seventeen, I left the town in the desert for a city in the desert. There were three million people in that city. There were a lot of straight, wide roads, and there weren't many sidewalks. Though I lived and worked elsewhere more than I lived and worked in that city, I always returned—each time for a different reason. When I left six weeks ago, I didn't tell anybody I was leaving. I just went to the airport one morning and got on a flight. I didn't even really pack. I had a few books and half a dozen shirts and toiletries and some other things. I wanted to live in a cold city. I couldn't say precisely why I picked this one.

I bought an ugly winter coat and found a cheap room at a place called Hotel Rus: This is where I'm living now. In the corridor there is a toilet that our floor shares, and a bathroom with a tiny but very deep tub I'm not sure how to use—am I supposed to stand or squat or sit in it? My room has green carpeting and white walls. It has a little sink and a mirror, a wardrobe, a little chest of drawers, and a small single bed. My feet dangle off the edge, and the duvet is too small. There's no TV, and that's fine with me. Sometimes I catch a bit of TV in a bar, and it looks pretty depressing. And I haven't come all this way to watch TV. The man and woman who run the place are nice, Mr. and Mrs. Pyz. One night they asked why I'd come and I said I didn't know. How long was I staying? I didn't have any plans to leave, I told them. But I was American, they said; I had to leave. I had a second passport, I told them. That's an old story.

A guy I knew from college had come here—he went to Europe and I went to the Navy. I had a number and an address, twenty years old. I'm sure he left nineteen years ago and went back home, and I don't remember liking him anyway. But on my first morning I bought a map and I walked many hours in the rain and fog to get to where my friend used to live. I needed an excuse to go somewhere specific. I could have got a bus or a streetcar or the subway, but I wanted to walk, and I suppose I was a bit frightened I'd get on the wrong train, the wrong bus, not have the right change, not know how to use the machines, be asked for directions, and I didn't want to look like a tourist. So I walked. It took a long time and my feet were sore. I thought about getting some new shoes the next day, but it wasn't until the day after the night I met Saskia and we stood around on cobblestones listening to musicians in the city center—it was a street festival—that I set out looking for a shoe store. I passed an outdoor adventure place and saw a lot of boots in the windows. I looked around and realized just about everybody on the slushy street was wearing boots. So I went inside and bought the most expensive pair they had: tall, black aqua combats—that's what they were called, aqua combats. I'm glad I waited. Had I bought them after that first walk, I might have got cheap ones. I wouldn't have considered the possibility that good shoes were essential: In the city I came from, shoes are never essential. Every week you buy a new pair of flip-flops at a drugstore for a dollar ninety-nine. I can step in a puddle with the boots I bought here. I can stand in a puddle for as long as I like. Every time I lace them up in the mornings, I'm glad I spent the extra money.

I wake up, usually around seven, and go and get a few papers, even though I can't read them, and a pack of cigarettes. I go back to the hotel and sit at the bar, or sometimes I go to a little café down on the corner where a nice young Italian guy waits tables, and he speaks English with me. He asks what I'm reading. He doesn't have the language either, not well enough to read it, so we both take guesses. He's into mobile phones and sunglasses, but he's a nice guy. He got me a free phone that I top up whenever I want to make a call. I spend about an hour with the papers. Then I go to the bakery next door to the café and get some sandwiches on nice bread, pack them into a little backpack, and start walking around the city. I tell myself it's been six weeks; perhaps it's been a little longer. Time is losing shape. Sometimes I watch my cigarette smoke rise above me in my hotel room and disperse across the ceiling, and this is what is happening to time. I am trying to live without a preoccupation with endpoints.

Saskia telephones from the front of the hotel. My phone rings on the little nightstand. I'm supposed to be ready. I've been up, thinking these things, about boots and the desert and ice, for hours, smoking and thinking. I had no idea it was so late, that I'd been lying here so long. I will take a shower quickly, I say to her. Come up to the room. She comes up and sits on my bed and stares at the wall. Saskia is twenty-five. She has dark black hair and brown eyes. She is small and a bit stocky. I come back from the shower and she sits patiently while I shave, brush my teeth, and dress. There is a moment when we both realize that I am getting dressed right in front of her, and I move a little toward one corner and she turns her head a little toward the opposite corner until I am finished. She has a newspaper with her, and has circled a dozen ads for apartments. Hotel Rus is a nice place, but it's still a hotel. I'd like a kitchen and a balcony, and my own bathroom. To get an apartment I'll need a bank statement, which I have—I opened up an account soon after I arrived, and wired myself money from the US— but I don't have any references, which means I'll get asked for a hefty deposit. So I put on a money belt that goes under my shirt, and stuff a lot of cash into it. Saskia is wearing a gray skirt over black tights and tall black boots, and a thick black sweater. She's always well dressed, but not always in the same way. Today she looks conservative. How many places are we going to see? I ask. We'll go to a café and make some phone calls, she says. You look tired, I say. She yawns. I *am* tired, she says. Saskia takes a lot of pills and goes to gigs and attends parties that last three days. She can't sleep. Her heart races and she wakes up in the middle of the night and goes for a run in the city. Is that dangerous? I asked once. I don't know, she said. I met her in a museum—in the National Gallery. She goes there for her lunch breaks. She works at an economics research institute; she expends a lot of energy every day on this and talks about it only if I ask her a direct question. She likes art and books and music, and that's what she wants to talk about. She has a small collection of paintings in her bedroom that she's told me about. Each one has an interesting history.

Propped up on the chest of drawers in my hotel room is a small painting that we bought together, and Saskia stares curiously at it. It's called *Untitled 14*. I bought it at an opening in the city center about a week after Saskia and I first met. Saskia goes to openings all the time. She drinks free wine, talks with the artists, and imagines an alternative life in which she is rich enough to become a collector. The artist we had seen that night was a woman on the verge of fame, said Saskia, which meant that her works were unaffordable, or affordable only to the wealthy. After we had walked around the gallery, silently, for about fifteen minutes, Saskia asked me what I thought. I thought the paintings were magnificent, I said, but I had a hard time explaining why. Which is your favorite? she asked. Which is yours? I asked. She pointed to the painting that is now in my hotel room. Mine too, I said. I asked her if she'd let me buy it for her. Absolutely not, she said. It's too expensive. It's not that expensive, I said. She suggested that I buy it for myself and my new apartment, when I found an apartment, and she would come over often to admire it. I agreed. Saskia handled the transaction, and we had a long conversation with the artist, which I did not understand at all, but I smiled and nodded when the artist looked at me. I put down a sizable cash deposit and agreed to come by the next day to settle up. That evening, after the opening, when Saskia and I went for a drink at a hotel bar that overlooked, from five stories up, a busy intersection, she asked what I did for a living. I said I did nothing. Is that the truth? she asked. I do nothing *now*, I said. She asked what I did before I did nothing and I told her I'd been in the Navy. She seemed to accept that I didn't want to say anything else, so she asked no more questions that night. A few days later I came back from a day's walking and found Mr. and Mrs. Pyz looking very happily at the painting, which had been delivered to the hotel, though it was still packed in brown paper.

Do you still like it? I ask, meaning the painting. Yes, very much, says Saskia. She smiles and rubs her knees. It's strange, since we only met a little while ago, to be in a hotel room together, getting ready to search for apartments like we are old friends. We act as though we ought to have things to talk about, but we don't have those things. We have fallen into a swift intimacy of pure circumstance. Sitting together on the bed now as I lace up my boots it occurs to me how easily this intimacy could evaporate. Our relationship probably could not bear any conflict at all. The force that stabilizes the intimacy is politeness. She is always polite, and I am always polite. Will we go now?

she asks. Would you like to? She looks out the window. It's pretty nasty outside. The snow is wet and gray, and there's a strong breeze, so strong that when it blows, my window rattles. I like to walk around in the snow because I'm still not used to it, but she grew up with it, so to her it's a nuisance. Yes, she says, let's go.

I put on my coat. She puts on a gray coat and a gray hat. She grabs her bag and has the folded newspaper under her arm. It was supposed to be clear today, she says. I open the door for her, and before she exits she walks to the painting, lifts it, turns it upside down — which is to say right side up, I realize — and replaces it on the chest. Oh, I say. It's hard to tell, she says. We walk into the corridor and see a Japanese man — one of my neighbors — walking to the shower. He is in a white bathrobe and big blue plastic shower slippers, and holds his clothes in a folded stack with both hands, and on top of the stack is a thin brown belt as well as some toiletries. Saskia goes by him without lifting her head, and he does not look at her. I find that people here are always reassuring each other that they exist and life exists and the city itself exists by refusing to communicate. I have lived beside the Japanese man for a few weeks, and we have started to give each other restrained greetings.

Saskia and I get into the elevator. It's just about big enough for the two of us. It smells like potpourri, and after you leave you smell like potpourri for a while, and if you live here long enough, and take the elevator often enough, you begin to smell potpourri in your dreams. I go in first, because Saskia has opened the door for me. We are facing each other, and the metal door with a little window in it swings shut. She presses the button and we begin to descend. This is an old elevator, one that doesn't have an inner door, so you can see the rough cement walls inside the building between floors as you descend. Saskia finally turns so that we are not face-to-face so close together. I am a whole foot taller than her, maybe more. On the night that we walked around the city in the cold, she linked her arm in mine and pressed very close—it was bitterly cold—and I had to take small steps to match her stride. The elevator is creaking. It always creaks, but for some reason it is creaking louder than usual. I ought to say something, but before I can, she says, There are three places in good locations. We'll call them first. There are a dozen others farther out, but you want to start in the center. Thanks for helping out, I say; I'm sure I'd pick the first one I came across, then I'd see something later and regret it. She smiles. We stop with a crunch. The elevator bounces, and rises slowly up. The little green light illuminates, which means we're free to go, and Saskia opens the door.

The reception area is empty. It's just a booth with a buzzer. When you buzz it, you often have to wait five minutes before Mr. Pyz or Mrs. Pyz comes out smiling.

Mr. Pyz is a bald man with a large belly and Mrs. Pyz is a tall woman with a large, elegant nose. Opposite the reception booth is the door to the restaurant and café, but the main entrance to that is on the street. The walls have wooden baseboards and old wallpaper. The burgundy carpet is covered in stains, not because the place is dirty, but because the carpet is — or seems to be — so old. There's never a crowd of Americans or Canadians or Australians or Irish twentysomethings wearing backpacks and looking at maps in the reception hall or vomiting in the elevator. And nobody complains about slow service or about noise. This is a hotel for people on their own. In the evenings, the restaurant is busy with locals who come here for traditional food. Mrs. Pyz wears a traditional outfit that pushes her breasts out. It gets really loud from about eight to eleven, and then all at once it goes quiet, except on Friday nights, when a blues band comes in. I went to see the band once, and it was hard to stay. I left after three or four songs. It's hard to watch European men sing the blues. They take it seriously, but the more seriously they take it, the more absurd they become. These guys knew a lot about the blues, they mentioned some good people, but their knowledge was dry. It wasn't ever going to be anything else. In their sound, there was an emptiness where inheritance ought to be. They manufactured black accents and spoke in broken English, and I felt a little embarrassed for them, so I left. I don't begrudge them. It was how they chilled out, and how they paid tribute to music they liked. The place was packed. All the tables were full, and some people stood. Mr. Pyz asked me what I thought about it the next morning. There was a time in my life when I would have wanted to say it was terrible, but that time has passed. I told him it was a lot of fun. Mr. Pyz is a nice man, and he's proud of his hotel. And Mrs. Pyz seems proud of Mr. Pyz.

Saskia is ahead of me, and gets to the door first. She turns around and makes a face. The face says, This is going to be painful. She pulls her shoulders together. Saskia can move quickly from being very cool to being very funny. It makes me think she's not trying to be one or the other. I wish we could preserve our relationship as it is now for a long time. I wish we could remain strangers. She opens the door. The street is white and the sky is a dark gray. We are met by an iciness that is even more intense than I expect, even though it is probably no different from yesterday's. Saskia digs in her bag for gloves, and I put a winter hat on and pull it down over my ears, as far down as I can get it. I zip my coat and turn the collar up, and stick my hands in my pockets. The subway station, where I buy my newspapers and cigarettes, is to the left. The bus is closer—it's to the right—but stops often on the way into the center. Which way, I say, the subway or the bus? It doesn't matter, she says. Cars go by with lights on, and the lights make the snow shine, and the way the light crawls up the street makes the snow appear to rise rather than fall. Saskia says, Maybe the bus is better. Her teeth are chattering. The shelter is closer, she says. We hurry down the sidewalk, through two trenches of stomped-down slush, created by foot traffic, in a thick layer of snow. Because it's a bit slippery and I'm trying to keep up with Saskia, I have to take my hands out of my pockets. My fingers start to go numb. My eyes have started to water and the water has started to freeze. I think in my entire life I've experienced this kind of cold once before, in Chicago, when I was visiting an old friend. I hated the cold there but I don't mind it here. It feels like I am walking through my own imagination now, or a dream.

The bus stop is beside the little café where the Italian kid works, but he's not there today, because it's Saturday. I'm hungry, but I don't want to delay us. I don't want to walk inside and order a piece of bread, and watch the bus go by. The bus arrives every fifteen minutes on a Saturday, and that's a lot of time in weather like this. A sick feeling rolls through my stomach, which is hunger, so I decide to smoke a cigarette. I pull the pack from my coat pocket and show it to Saskia. She says, Okay, but you light it; I'm not taking my gloves off. So I light hers, then my own. I have often wondered when, if at all, I might consider quitting, but now that I am here I have decided there's no point. It would be different if I had a family, or if I played a sport. But all I do now is walk, and I don't want to live an especially long time.

From the top of the street, coming slowly, is a blue bus — our bus. The traffic is slow because of the weather. The roads are fine, but the visibility is poor. Saskia smokes the cigarette I have lit for her without hands, just holding it between her lips, breathing in and breathing out. She crosses her arms and looks down the street, at the bus, which is stuck in the traffic it towers over, wipers moving slowly across its windshield, and the whole scene is white and gray and lit up and smoking. I don't know how long we wait. It is probably a minute, but it feels like ten. Saskia is thinking that we should have taken the subway, and I can see that she wants to say something about this, but also that she doesn't want to complain. I say, I wonder if the place I get will have a balcony. Do you want a balcony? she asks. I'd like one. That would make our list smaller, she says. It's not a necessity, I say.

Finally the bus stops in front of us. I take a seat by the window and wipe a streak in the fogged glass so we can see outside, and Saskia sits beside me. And the bus departs, and we watch the street through this small aperture, and we don't speak. I worry that she may find me too quiet, or boring. I could fill the silence by talking about the past, but I try not to think about the past. For much of my life, I existed in a condition of regret, a regret that was contemporaneous with experience, and which sometimes preceded experience. Whenever I think of my past now I see a great black wave that has risen a thousand stories high and is suspended above me, as though I am a city by the sea, and I hold the wave in suspension through a perspective that is as constrained as a streak of clear glass in a fogged-up window.

Saskia takes her gloves and hat off. I pull the collar of my coat down and pull my winter hat off. She looks at me and says, I don't think I'm ever getting off this bus. Saskia has a dark complexion. Her eyes look very tired, and the circles under them are blue sometimes, in certain light. I used to have trouble sleeping. It wasn't anything in particular, just a fear that I ought to be doing something, that something needed being done, or that something was wrong. I had bad dreams. The dreams were often about showing up to places unprepared, or being asked to do something that I didn't know how to do. And other times I just lay there, twisting and rearranging pillows, or got up for a glass of water and then stood by the window for a while. But I sleep now. I've never slept like I sleep here. I never believed this kind of sleep was possible. I am forty-one years old. I don't drink as much as I used to. I hardly drink at all here. I like to be awake in the mornings, and thinking clearly. My alarm goes off at seven and I lie in bed for a while. I feel rested. I feel like I've been asleep for ten years. I smoke cigarettes and listen to the street. I read a book. The book I'm reading now is something Saskia gave me, an old book of sights to see in the city, with some historical information. The print is tiny and the translation is bad. It says things like, You are pleasing to see the statue. I'm going to learn the language and buy some novels soon. I want to read very long and old ones. They don't have to be great. I'm going to buy a chair that's comfortable, and when it's cold I'm going to set it by the window, and when it's warm I'm going to pull the chair onto my balcony, if I have one, and read outside in the sunshine, and listen to birds. I am also going to listen to the radio, and I hope my balcony will look over some trees and a street, one where people honk their horns at each other.

When is the last time you slept? I ask her. She doesn't know. Weeks, she guesses, maybe never. She pauses. I don't mean never, she says, just that it feels like never. She yawns. You're making me tired now, she says. Can I see the newspaper? I ask. She hands it to me. It's damp. I peruse the ads she has circled. I realize my mistake and hand the paper back to her. Saskia could have telephoned these places from my hotel room, or she could call them now, but she doesn't. It's the whole experience she wants. We shall sit in a café and have some coffee or tea and she'll make calls there, then plan our route. I like that we're not rushing anything, that everything is pointlessly ritualized. The bus is beginning to fill now. Bodies begin to push backward, and a man with a backpack bumps Saskia on the head. She rolls her eyes. That was nice of him, I say. The man turns around and gives me a dirty look, a look that says, Where am I supposed to go? So I give him a look that says, You could at least remove your backpack. Saskia, realizing I've become perturbed, says, to me, You must be used to lots of space. The guy mumbles something. I ignore it. I can't speak the language. I'd look like a fool if I tried to start an argument, and anyway it might be the wrong argument. The man turns back around and Saskia gets hit by the backpack again, so she quickly and quietly unzips its small back pocket. Revenge, she whispers. The reason the bus is getting crowded on a Saturday morning is that everyone is going into the center to shop, and to visit Christmas markets and drink and have cakes. The economy is bad, but there is only this weekend and the next before Christmas. The streak I wiped in the glass beside me has fogged up again, so I wipe it again. I realize we are moving fast now—we must be in a bus lane. This is a nice time of year, says Saskia, if you don't mind crowds. I say, Sometimes I like crowds. Good, she says, because it's going to be crowded. We cross a large suspension bridge, and the sound of the tires on the road changes considerably. The change nearly creates the sensation of floating. My ears pop. Saskia leans across me to wipe a larger streak in the glass. A long way below is the river, wide and black. The surface of the river is choppy, and snow is falling everywhere, in many directions.

We reach the other side, after a long minute, and the sound of the tires on the road changes back, and we are in the immediate outskirts of the center now. The buildings here are all the same. You walk along one street, turn a corner, and you are on the same street. This is what the foreigner tells himself. The longer I stay here, though, the more I notice imperfections in the repetition. I notice a laneway here or there that is small and winding, a shortcut. Or an alley that leads to a street that it seemingly shouldn't, which tells you that your inner compass has failed. Or you notice a little gateway that leads to a square. Or there's an old monastery. Or a man who always sweeps the sidewalk outside his shop. You begin to notice that no two buildings are really alike. You begin to see that what you suspected was perfect repetition in an orderly grid is apparent repetition in an imperfect grid, and after a while you learn that what you once considered monolithic is infinitely intricate. And from here you begin to understand the vastness of the place.

The bus stops at a hub for streetcars, trains, and buses that come in from the west, across the bridge. Is this us? I ask. Saskia is yawning again. The bus is really warm now. Everyone has been breathing, and creating heat. No, she says, we have a few more stops. The doors open and the bus almost empties. The heat is released with the people who alight. It is sucked immediately into the morning, and what's left in the bus is cold and refreshing space.

Where are we going? I ask. Saskia says, A café with lots of students. It's…and she pauses, seemingly searching for the correct English word. It's the first time since I met her that she has paused for a word, and this makes me momentarily wonder at how impressive it is that she speaks English so well. Her accent sounds a bit British. Did you live in England? I asked her once. No, she said. But we study English here for a long time. I studied Spanish in high school and college, I said. *Habla español?* she asked. Not a word, I answered. She taught herself Latin, so she could read Virgil in the original. She is now reading Dante in Italian, and hopes to learn Japanese next. This is a girl who also spends half her life at parties.

I wipe the window again to see where we are. The closer we get to the center, the more Christmaslike the city gets. I don't mind too much about spending Christmas in a hotel. But I would like a little more space. As much as I like Mr. and Mrs. Pyz, I'd like to have a life where people don't monitor my movements, even accidentally. I'd like to have my own pots and pans. I'd like a table to place a bowl of fruit on. I have an idea of myself walking around markets where butchers and grocers shout prices over the crowds, and where I'll carefully and slowly choose vegetables and meat, and come home to cook myself meals. I'd like to have breakfast without having to get dressed. I'd like to wander in and out of rooms and take a bath with the door open. And I don't want to look out the window of a little room and wonder where, in the city, I'll end up. The most essential quality of hotel life is the thing I want least: a presumption of departure.

Saskia peers forward and hits the button on the rail. There's a pleasing *ding*, and a light illuminates near the driver that says the bus is going to stop. This is us, says Saskia. She puts her hat and gloves back on and stands. The bus pulls over into the gray slop that snowplows and traffic have driven toward the curb and comes to a halt. The door opens. Saskia hops out and I follow. I put my hat on and zip up my coat and put my hands back in my pockets. The unlit Christmas lights stretched above the street are rocking in the wind. They could easily light them — it is dark enough. Are you hungry? I ask. Not really, she says, are you? I am, I say. I think I ought to eat something straightaway. Are we far from the café? Ten or fifteen minutes, she says. Okay, I say, then let me just get a quick snack. Right beside us there's a stand that serves fish fingers and fish sandwiches. These stands are everywhere, and they're not bad. They load the sandwiches up with mayonnaise and lime juice and fresh coriander, and the bread is usually fresh. I'd never heard of anything like fish sandwiches from street vendors before I came here, and for that reason I eat them all the time.

I eat while we walk. Saskia suggests we stop so I don't get a stomachache, but I know she's only being nice. It's too cold to stand still. I eat the whole thing in four bites, so that I can put my hands back in my pockets. The first three bites are small, but I take the whole last half of the sandwich with the fourth, and have to cover my face with my hands. You eat like an animal, she says. I chew and chew and hold my finger up, indicating that I'm chewing. I always used to eat quickly, but lately I have been sitting at dinner tables in restaurants and cafés, and after I swallow a bite I put my fork and knife or spoon down and allow a thought to rise to the surface — one that is purely philosophical, that is in no way actionable, and that relaxes the mind.

The fish sandwich makes me feel better immediately. I throw the packaging into a trash can, wipe my mouth and hands with a napkin, and throw that into the can. Then I take a drink of water. Okay, I say. Okay, says Saskia. She leads us to the left, onto a short, narrow street with a lot of closed-down old shops. The foot or two of sidewalk separating the buildings from the road is not wide enough for both of us, or either of us, in fact, so we walk on the road, which is white and soft and thick with snow. I used to live near here, and take this street to the café, says Saskia; we're very near the university. At that moment a car appears behind us and honks. It's a polite honk, a short honk, just to let us know it's there. And that's when I first realize that the wind is howling. You cannot even hear cars that are a few feet behind you. Saskia steps out of the way and I file behind her. The car goes by, an old silver Mercedes driven by a man with huge silver hair. My face is wet and feels hard because it's so numb. I move alongside Saskia again. She has her arms crossed and walks with her head pointed down. The street is ascending. The Mercedes, ahead of us, is sliding all over the place.

I was thinking about taking some language courses, I say. Saskia contemplates this by looking up, lifting her chin. This is what she does when she contemplates something. That's a good idea, she says. Would you like me to help you find one? I say, Hmm, and I nod my head, because I cannot say no without feeling rude and I cannot say yes without embarrassment. I'm embarrassed that she's doing all the favors and I offer nothing in return. I sense this doesn't bother her, and she knows I have nothing to offer. Nothing in the way of assistance, anyway. Nothing in the way of information, or a practicality. I alleviate a kind of loneliness in her, perhaps. I give her somebody else to fret about. Or she is simply being hospitable. Or all of these things.

She stops to examine a building. For a moment she says nothing. Her arms stay crossed. She blinks a lot, because snowflakes are getting into her eyes. This place, she says, used to be famous. Yes? I say. I examine it with her. Its windows are boarded up. The stone façade is rain-stained, but that makes it like every other building on the street. Maybe it's another one, says Saskia. She scans up and down the street, looking slightly bewildered. There used to be a famous little book press on this street, she says. They published lots of anarchist novels. The publisher was jailed. But that was a hundred years ago. Then it became a famous bookshop. Sort of famous. It was where people went when they wanted to pretend to be anarchists. When did it close? I ask. When I was very young, she says. Not enough people wanted to pretend to be anarchists. We stand for ten seconds longer, and then she says, But I can't remember which building it was.

We continue up the hill, walking side by side. The street leads to a stairway that zigzags up a ridge, then opens onto a wide platform with a sculpture on it, something abstract and large, two curved shapes, one stacked on top of the other. What's it supposed to be? I ask. It is a memorial for massacred Jews, she says. That is a mother embracing the corpse of a child. After about thirty seconds, during which we kneel to get a look at the child, we continue onward. There's another short stairway at the other end of the platform. It's not far now, she says. At the top of the stairway we find ourselves on another small gray street. The street is empty of vehicles or people. There's a light in a window not far from us. A door opens, and suddenly there is a lot of noise, and an orange light. A couple steps out, the door closes behind them, and the sound dissolves and the light disappears. And now I can hear the couple speaking, but I don't understand what they're saying. The woman is catching the snow in her mittens. That's the café, says Saskia. She looks both ways and starts to cross the street. The surface is slippery, and Saskia throws her arms out for balance when she nearly slips. I take her arm and we help each other cross. The street is so narrow that the surface probably never sees direct sunlight in winter. I don't recognize the street. It seems strange that I have walked so many hours in this city and still don't recognize places. I tend to begin my walks in places I know—I never fling myself completely into unfamiliarity—and move outward slowly, turning this way and that, and try to find my way back. I almost always do. Then I find a new point of origin and do it all over again. I also like shortcuts, so I test tiny alleyways that wind away from bigger streets. I open gates. I crawl under small archways that appear to lead nowhere, but often take you to interesting spots. I walk through sleepy private gardens and grounds. The stairs and the memorial and now the café—I get a lot of pleasure out of the secrecy of this city. This is something Saskia and I have in common.

She opens the door for me. We are met by the sound of voices and the smell of coffee. The café is warm and stretches back a long way, through an archway into a second room. The walls are covered with posters—scenes of city life and reproductions of old masterpieces. There is one of a nude man, covering his genitals with his hands, wearing a donkey mask. The booths are red velvet. The tables and chairs are dark brown wood. There are immense chandeliers, and the waiters are dressed in tuxedos. There aren't any free tables in the front room. Saskia tells me to wait while she checks the back. She takes off her hat and gloves and unbuttons her coat. She stuffs her gloves and hat into her coat pocket and, on the way to the back room, hangs the coat on a rack. I unzip my coat and take off my hat. I wait where Saskia told me to wait. She disappears into the second room. Through the archway I see that the second room, the back room, is much larger than the front, but not as nice. The tables are fold-out tables, covered in oilcloth, and the chairs are cheap. It looks just as packed as the front room. A minute passes, maybe more. A waiter begs my pardon, not apologetically but as a warning that I could be trampled, as he goes to a table with drinks and again on the way back, with an armful of plates. I am in his way.

I put my hat in my coat pocket and take my coat off and hang it on the coatrack, then I walk through the archway. Saskia is standing by a table, talking to a guy. He looks about her age around the eyes, but he has a huge scruffy beard that makes him seem older. He sees me looking at Saskia, and she turns and waves me over. I don't really like the idea of having to meet somebody, especially a young man with an old beard, but she seems happy to see him. I walk over, she introduces me to him — his name is Janos—and we shake hands. American? he says. That's right, I say. Where in America? he asks. Delaware, I say. That's what I say to everybody. He nods. Saskia asks if I mind joining him while we phone around for apartments. Not at all, I say. Janos gets the attention of the waiter. Saskia orders a tea and a bun. I order a coffee and a piece of cake. You learn to say some things quickly in a foreign language. You learn what to call your favorite types of food. You learn to say please and thank you. You learn to place orders—that is, you learn to say, *I would like* instead of *I want*. Janos is small, with round, drooping shoulders, but handsome eyes and nose. He is having a small beer and some soup. He takes a drink and froth gets stuck in his mustache. There's some soup in the bottom of his beard. Saskia speaks to Janos in English, but he doesn't answer her in English. She's telling him about the apartment. Then he says something, something obviously about her relationship to me. I can see immediately this is a kind of jealousy that is based on national propriety rather than love. I say, So, Janos, what's happening? He looks at Saskia. I say, What are you doing today? Shopping for Christmas presents, he says. That's nice, I say. Then he says something to Saskia. She answers sharply, and then there is silence.

I'd prefer, if such a thing were possible, or perhaps I mean if I were patient enough, to teach myself the language: get some books, go read them in dark, quiet libraries, listen to some CDs, eavesdrop on streetcars, in cafés, and so on. I'd prefer to stay out of classrooms, avoid learning by exercises, chapters, and tests. But I need to make haste. I create an alarming foreignness wherever I go. In a year I'd like to be invisible. I'd like to sit down at tables with strangers and not be an interruption, or a curiosity. I want to walk into a barbershop and get a haircut and speak two or three sentences about the weather and pay and leave, and be so inconspicuous that the barber immediately forgets I was there. For this I will need not only language but accent, so I am studying the sounds of people, even if I don't understand what they're saying, and on my walks I repeat them to myself. If I know I am completely alone, I say them out loud. You are looking for a place to live? asks Janos. That's right, I say. For how long? he asks. I don't know, I say. Probably for a while. Saskia puts the newspaper in front of Janos so he can read the ads she has circled. He looks them over. He shakes his head at some, but is impressed by the look of others. You must be rich, he says. I've saved, I say. What did you do? he asks. I was in the Navy, I say, partly because I figure Saskia may already have told him, and I don't want to be caught in a lie, and partly because I want to obliterate the possibility that Janos and I will become friends. He smiles because he thinks I am joking. Then he stops smiling. It's too early for cake, he says. I say nothing. I never had a taste for sweet things before, but now I do. Now I really like to eat rich, sweet, fruity, creamy cakes, and it doesn't matter what time of day it is. Janos finishes his soup and takes another drink of his beer. He wants to say something. I can see it in his eyes. He leans forward. He almost speaks. Then he leans back.

Saskia makes her first phone call. She holds her thumb, which is, here, the same as crossing one's fingers. She waits, and waits, and waits, and frowns, then leaves a message. Then she draws a star by the ad. Our food comes. Saskia dials another number. She waits. And waits. She frowns again, and shakes her head at me when she gets to voicemail. She leaves a short message. She draws a star by the ad and says, It's December, it's the worst time to look. She dials the next number on the list and someone answers. Excitedly, she grabs my arm. She speaks. She is, perhaps, trying to explain the situation, who I am, that I am an American — I hear the word *American*. Her telephone voice is not like her regular voice. It is severe, professional, and lacks empathy, and I find it totally incongruous with the fact that her hand is on my arm, that she is excited. Then she's cut off in the middle of a sentence, or what seems like the middle of a sentence. She frowns and says good-bye. It's gone already, she says. She draws a line through the ad. Pity, she says. It had a balcony. Maybe you should not tell landlords I'm American, I say. Saskia dismisses this.

She pauses to eat and drink. This is exciting, she says.

I'm excited, too, I say. And we all eat and drink for a bit. It is true that I'm excited, but I also feel relief that we may not find an apartment, that I can go on living in a hotel for a month or two, that I can continue to eat all my meals in restaurants and cafés, and sleep on a tiny bed in a small room with nothing at all by way of decoration, except the one painting. I'm ashamed of this feeling that I might be quite content in the shallow, purgatorial waters of hotel life. My cake is full of warm raspberries and warm blackberries and is covered in cream. Janos eyes it suspiciously, as do other diners around us. I'm wearing my boots, jeans, a black belt, a blue T-shirt, and a dark brown, button-down shirt with long sleeves. I bought the brown shirt here, and a few others just like it, because all my shirts made me feel conspicuously American. I'm also letting my hair grow. My US passport photo shows me with neat, clean, and well-groomed hair, tapered above the ears and around the neck from the lower natural hairline upward at least three-fourths of an inch and outward not greater than three-fourths of an inch to blend with hairstyle, et cetera. The photo was taken just after I left the Navy. I look at it sometimes, while lying in bed, and it's like I am staring at a picture of a dead brother. I didn't really know him, but I know he had hopes. I know he was a well-behaved young boy once, and that he was smart, a straight-A student who never had to study, but studied constantly, and dreamed of being a leader. But he is dead now. He died unexpectedly.

When Saskia has finished half her bun, she wipes her hands, pours herself another cup of tea from the pot, and picks up the phone again. How many are left? I ask. There are plenty, but not too many in the center. That doesn't matter much to me, I say. It does, she says, you want to live in the center. Janos says, Saskia wants a friend who lives in the center. Saskia says, Everybody wants a friend who lives in the center. Okay, I say, I don't mind. She makes another call. There's no answer. She leaves a message and draws a star by the ad. Well, I say, what now? She tells me she's tried all the best places. Maybe they'll call back, I say. I doubt it, says Janos, that's the Thursday paper. Is there a paper from today we can check? I ask. There is, Saskia says, but the list of apartments will be very small—the Thursday paper is the one to buy. But only if you go looking on Thursday, says Janos. I got my apartment on a Saturday, says Saskia. Janos nods, because she has proved his point: Your apartment is small and full of mice, he says. It's not full of mice! says Saskia. Well, the stairwell is full of mice, says Janos. Saskia gets up. Where are you going? I ask. To get today's paper, she says. I'll go with you, I say. She doesn't want me to. She puts her hand out as though she is a policewoman and I am traffic, and she apologizes for having an old paper. She's upset about it. I don't mind, I say. What's the difference between getting an apartment now and getting an apartment in January? It's my fault for waiting so late in the first place. She sits down. It's ridiculous that they print the ads on a Thursday, when everyone has to work, she says. We could telephone some of the places that are outside the center? No, I say, let's just wait. Maybe they'll call back.

She goes to the bathroom and I am left on my own with Janos. He watches her weave between the tables, so I turn and watch her as well. In the image of this pretty, well-dressed girl, who is an economist, and whom I met just weeks ago, walking through a crowd of chairs and tables and artists in a loud, warm, and smoke-filled café in a cold city I never considered visiting until I moved here forever, having no concept of the meaning of forever anyway, I attain a state of weightlessness, as though I am in deep space. This happens many times a day here, and I try to clear my mind of the desire to wonder why it arrives, and what it means, or if it means anything at all. In the mornings, in my tiny bed, in my small, undecorated room, I lie very still, and I replace the naked scenery of that room with the memories of my new unfamiliarity. I lie there and ponder these memories for a long time, and even though it is cold and blowing outside, my room is warm. There is a hot radiator just below the window. When I come back from the shower, I open up the window to freshen the room, and I wait for it to get cold again, and then I close the window and dress.

You should not tell anyone that you were in the Navy, says Janos. I turn around and see him sitting in an aggressive but also embarrassed posture over his empty beer. There is still foam on his mustache and soup in his beard. People don't like Americans in the first place, he says. I say, That's true. Did you fight? What do you mean? I mean in a war, he says. Iraq, I say. Iraq? Yes, I say. You must tell no one that, he says. It's behind me, I say. I never think about it. Tell no one, he repeats. The waiter walks by, so I tell him I'd like to pay — this too you learn quickly, how to say you'd like to pay. He does not register that he has heard me, but they usually don't. They move like stone chess pieces through fog. It shows a lack of refinement to initiate contact with waiters in cafés like this one, where the whole point of being here is to prove that you are not in a hurry. You must learn to wear an attitude of being ready to pay, or wanting another drink, or being ready to order, and they simply come to you. There's a degree of mysticism about it. But I haven't learned the secret, so I just hold up my hand and say the words as they pass. They usually come back a few minutes later and tally up the prices of the things I've ordered — this is done on paper — and tell me the total, and when they realize I have not understood, they place their sums in front of me and I give them some cash. I leave a tip on the table, even though you are supposed to include it when you pay. I do this because I do not know how to tell them to take extra for a tip. I watch the way people around me handle the transaction, with as little conversation as possible. I say nothing else to Janos, and he decides to check his phone for messages, and a few minutes pass. I look around the room and watch other people talking. The volume of the place has gone up, or maybe it's just that I'm paying attention to the noise. A few more minutes pass. Saskia comes out of the door to the toilets. We are looking at each other before we realize we are looking at each other. I turn around. She's back, I say to Janos. He lifts his head up from his phone. Saskia pulls out her chair and sits down as the waiter returns. He adds up the cost and tells me a number, and I give him a note that is easily large enough to cover it. Saskia tries to give me some money. You pay next time, I say. Fine, she says. In America, a person who says *fine* is pissed off with you, but here it expresses something like *great*, or *cool*. The waiter counts out change, and Janos asks him for another beer. There is no response, but Janos doesn't need one. I hate shopping, he says. Maybe I'll just stay here for the day.

Saskia and I stand at the same time. I'm happy we're going to be on our own again. I'm happy we're going to be walking again. Maybe we'll see you later? Saskia says to Janos. Perhaps, says Janos. Good luck finding an apartment, he says. Thanks, I say. Good-bye. Good-bye, he says. Good-bye, says Saskia. Saskia motions for me to go first. She holds her arm out as though she is an usher directing me to my seat in a theater. She is always doing this, always escorting me through places, opening doors for me, or paying for drinks. I also open doors for her, and I help her put her coat on, sometimes. I see lots of men doing this here, so I do it. I like doing it. Here, in this city, intense joy and intense sorrow are extinct. The place is too old for that kind of naïveté. Everyone here responds to these extinctions by opening doors for each other, or making room at tables—they are generous and polite. I admire this—to celebrate the extinction of hope with ritual and composure. To place coats on the shoulders of women. There isn't a thought left. There isn't a sentence. There isn't a human being. Janos has a beard because it is the embodiment of the hope that he is not recycled matter, that he has thoughts that are his own. He will wake up one day, maybe a year from now, or five, and shave it. I take Saskia's coat off the rack and she walks toward me and turns around, and puts her arms into the sleeves, and we leave the warm orange light of the café and return to the purple and white darkness of the street.

Janos is always unhappy, she says. It makes him happy to be unhappy. It must take so much effort to find unhappiness in everything. You're not unhappy? I ask. Oh, she says, I'm not stupid, but I don't make an effort to be unhappy.

The cold gets right into my lungs and refreshes me. The snow is coming down a little heavier than before. We turn right, into the wind and snow. We'll get a newspaper and check it for apartments, she says, and make our way into the center. She crosses her arms and I stick my hands in my pockets, and we walk very close together, so close that we bump into each other. I open a hole with my arm and she slots her arm through. If I were looking for an apartment, she says, I would like one with high ceilings and a big bathtub, and large windows facing a park. What about the kitchen? I ask. She contemplates this—again she lifts her head, like a philosopher. I don't cook well, she says. Do you? I like to cook, I say, and I'd like to have a nice kitchen. I have a small kitchen, she says. I hardly ever eat at home. My kitchen depresses me. I don't want a kitchen that depresses me, I say. The streets around here are somber and pretty. We begin to encounter other people. The road curves and widens. There are shops and cafés and a bank. And then there is a small intersection, and a bit of traffic. Saskia and I go inside a shop and she buys a newspaper. She tries to open the paper inside the shop, but it's a small space, tiny, and other people come in, so we have to leave.

We return to the cold and Saskia says there is something worth seeing nearby. It's something she's been wanting to show me since we met, but keeps forgetting. And now we are extremely close to it, so we must have a look. She links her arm in mine again, and walks a little more swiftly. I can't believe I keep forgetting this, she says. We turn onto another street, which is narrow, and which hooks sharply, and ascends. From here to the center, there is nothing but a slow ascent. This street is full of people just standing around. Someone is playing a trumpet, slowly and plaintively. We turn the corner and arrive at a small Christmas market in a square. There are brown huts full of Christmas ornaments, wooden children's toys, and jewelry. There is a stage where the man playing the trumpet stands. He's warming up. People are eating pretzels and doughnut balls covered in confectioners' sugar. They are drinking mulled wine. Parents have brought little children out in strollers. All you can see are little sleeping faces in beds of fur. Green turf has been laid all over the ground, but you see the green only where feet have stomped the snow into muddy slush. It is just like every other Christmas market I've come across, with minor differences. Is this what you wanted to show me? I ask. No, she says, this is. There's a small fountain in the middle of the square. In it, there's a statue of a man in a gown, with a halo over his head. Who's that supposed to be? I ask. That's a saint, says Saskia. Saint Nicholas — the saint of seafarers. She points to a brown Romanesque church that stands at one end of the square. That's the church he's buried in, in a catacomb, she says. We walk right up to the fountain, which is dry and full of soft snow. Around the feet of the saint, and leaping toward the edge, with their mouths open, are strange sea creatures. What do those look like? she asks. I think they look like a cross between a fish and a dragon, but I don't say it. They have stubby whiskers and massive fins. They have spikes on their tails like dinosaurs. They have huge round mouths with fangs. I say, I suppose they are mythological. Saskia shakes her head. I give them another look. They look to me like something a boy would draw — the scariest fish he could ever imagine. I try to imagine them a hundred times larger, and swimming in the ocean. I imagine the swell they create on the surface as they approach old ships full of terrified sailors. I give up, I say. They are dolphins, she says. Those aren't dolphins, I say. Well, they are supposed to be dolphins, she says, but the artist had never seen one. Are you sure that's true? It's true, she says. That's funny, I say. The fountain has a name, but everyone calls it the dolphin fountain. So did everyone go around hundreds of years ago thinking these were dolphins? I guess, says Saskia, or perhaps they immediately realized the artist was a fool. I nod. Saskia then says, What kind of boats were you on? In the Navy? I ask. Yes, she says, if you don't mind me asking. Submarines, I say.

The man playing the trumpet finally begins a Christmas song. It's quick and happy. I feel really glad to have happened upon this place. It always seems a degree or two warmer inside Christmas markets. There are space heaters in huts and crowds generating heat. Saskia joins a line outside the hut for drinks. She looks back at me. I have a funny feeling she has brought me here in order to place me in this shot — the sailor under the statue of the saint of seafarers, and the demonic dolphins. She smiles, then turns back to the hut and waits. I squat down to see the dolphins eye to eye. I don't think the sculpture really holds up as a work of art, but then again it is still here, and people are still, obviously, coming to look at it, not for the saint, I'd bet, but to marvel at the little dolphins, which are not dolphins at all, but examinations of the fantastic reality of human fear. Insofar as the statue is that, it's nice to look at.

Saskia returns with two mugs of hot wine. We light cigarettes. Do you think this is art? I ask. She says, Of course, why not? Well, I say, I guess I don't know. I never ask if anything is art, she says. If someone says something is art, I agree. She says this without changing the tone of her voice, as coolly as you could imagine. I don't know how to have a conversation about art, because nobody I have ever met, until Saskia, considered it worthy of serious discussion. I have thought about art but I have not tested my thoughts. Well, what if you think it's terrible? I ask. What does it matter if I think it's terrible? she says. I take a sip of my wine. She says, Bad artists trade on people's refusal to accept their work as art. I accept their work as art, so that there is nothing for their art to hide behind. That makes sense, I say.

The wine at Christmas markets can be way too sweet, and it can make you feel sick, but this wine is pretty much perfect. The snow blows all around Saskia, and around the huts, and up in the sky above the church. I switch my mug from one hand to the other, which has been warm and in my pocket, so I can put my cold hand in my pocket. The wine goes cold quickly, so you sip it for a bit, until you finish half, but then you must gulp the rest. Another? Saskia asks. No, I say, better not. I switch hands again with the mug. You need some gloves, she says, and takes the mug, so I can put both hands in my pockets. We leave the fountain and find a table under the large awning of one of the huts, and she takes the newspaper out. Okay, she says, and flattens out the page in front of us. See how much smaller the apartments section is on Saturdays? It's true. There are only two columns that run down half a page, whereas on Thursdays there are four full pages of ads. She runs her index finger down the columns as she reads. Here's one, she says. It's in the center. I try to read it but I can't understand it. Looks good, I say. She takes her phone out and pulls off her glove. She dials the number, holds the phone to her ear, and unbuttons the top of her coat. It's a gray wool coat with a thick collar and large buttons, and it falls just below her knees. It makes me want a new coat. Soon after I arrived, I walked into a disconsolate little shop by the train station, just a white room with coats on rolling racks, and a fat guy with a mustache started throwing coats at me, piling them in my arms. I didn't like anything. I tried to leave but he wouldn't let me. He kept dropping his price. He spoke English. He was an Arab. He'd made me as an American, and was telling me he wanted to get to America and see the West. There is nothing to see in the West, I said, except sky and dirt, though everybody there seems to be satisfied with that. People will tell you it's beautiful, and I suppose it must be, if it is to them. I told him I'd rather look around some more, that nothing in his shop was exactly what I wanted, and he grabbed me by the arm and told me I was making a mistake, that there was a coat for me there. He stood between me and the door, still with a creepy smile on his face, and I knew I would have to really assert myself to get away without buying something. I let him win. From now on, I am going to let everyone win. I picked up the most boring coat in the place and gave him his final offer. I put the coat on, zipped it up, and walked out the door, and the next day I walked by and the shop no longer existed. Mr. Pyz explained that this is common — these guys are just traders who sell out of spaces they use illegally for a day, or even a few hours. There are a lot of Arabs in the city, and a lot of Africans, and a lot of Roma, and everyone here seems to think they fill the place with stink and depravity — even Mr. and Mrs. Pyz, who are nice and decent people. Nobody in rich countries wants to face responsibility for the lives of people in poor countries. They just want cheap groceries. But now I am going on about something I don't want to think about. Everything human beings can imagine has been thrown at injustice, and injustice just absorbs it, and enlarges. Saskia is still on the phone. I stop thinking and watch her. She winks at me. The news must be good. The man on the trumpet finishes and there is soft and sustained applause. I look over at him. He takes off his hat as a salute. A good musician treats a small audience the same way he treats a large one, with humility and grace. A good musician does not play for glory. He plays to thank fortune for his ability. He plays to honor his predecessors. Saskia hangs up. Good news, she says. We can see it at two. She checks the time on her phone. We have a few hours, she says. I've decided I'd like to get a coat, I say. She likes this idea, and for the first time I understand that she doesn't like the coat I'm wearing, not at all. There are some department stores on the way to the apartment, she says.

The trumpet begins again. The music is faster now and people start dancing. Whatever makes people want to dance makes me want to stand completely still. This is how I appreciate good music. It makes me feel calm. I think Saskia is like this too. Her eyes are calm. She and I are just standing. It's nice to just stand and listen to music, to a single instrument. In the evenings, at the larger markets, big bands play. They belt out huge polka versions of pop songs, or sentimental old Christmas tunes, and those are a lot of fun too. The crowds stand around contentedly, drinking and listening to the music, and I walk slowly through them, politely making way for anybody crossing my path. The apartment has a terrace, says Saskia, and a big kitchen. I'll take it, I say. You haven't even seen it! Doesn't matter, I say. I think you should see it first. It could be full of mice. I'll get a cat, I say. It's expensive, she says. Well, then it probably doesn't have mice. I thought you said you weren't in a rush, she says. I have a good feeling, I say. She is weighing the risk of asking me another question, one that is much larger, but she resists. Do you really want to get a coat? she asks eventually. Yes, I say. We return our mugs to the drinks hut and get some money back. There is still dancing in front of the stage. Adults are dancing with their children and grandchildren. There you go, I say. What? she says. Now that's a picture, I say. Yes, but it's a pity when Christmas passes, and all we have left is the cold. I don't know, I say, I think I'd like a long winter. You'll get one, she says. Don't worry. We leave the market and the little square in front of the church, and the fountain with the saint of seafarers in it, and we press upward. From time to time, the center appears above and ahead of us, in the snow and fog and dimness, through spaces between building tops, spires, arches. We are heading for the interior. There is a cathedral there, and a fortress, but from here they are just faint shadows.

Saskia was born in this city. Both her parents are dead—the mother first and the father a few years after.

Her father was not from here, and when she was young she moved away. She came back after the death of her father, and I have the impression she came back in order to get a good job. She says there are two kinds of economists: the kind that own jets and the kind that ride bicycles. She doesn't seem to think of herself as a person who wants a jet, so I presume this makes her an economist on a bicycle. Except that when she is pushed to defend a position, or when she talks about the assumptions her colleagues make about her because she is a woman, for instance that she will eventually want a child more than she will want a promotion, she reveals an ambition to succeed not just because she can but because other people think she cannot, or would not.

Somebody here asked me about my politics. I told him I had none. We were sitting in a bar, and he was drinking, and I was not drinking, not really, just a beer, slowly, and he said I was a liar. His name was Fritz. Everything is political, said Fritz. I said nothing, and Fritz, I suppose, realized I had not agreed with him, so he told me what I really felt was disillusionment with politics, and that's not the same thing as having no politics. He seemed like a nice guy. We hung out for the rest of the night. He said, I don't smoke, but all night he smoked my cigarettes, and then we went to an automat so I could buy more cigarettes, and he said, Get me a pack too, so I bought him a pack. He put that pack in his pocket and smoked the cigarettes in my pack. He talked almost entirely about himself, and the city, and about politics. He was comically short and had a very funny walk, like something out of the Ministry of Silly Walks, where every step off his right foot was a bounce, as though he was trying to see over a short fence. He took me on a long walk that ended at the Parliament building, and there he shook my hand and said good-bye. Good-bye, I said, and I've never seen him since. Fritz. A good name. That was one of my first nights in the city. Or maybe it was recently. As time diffuses, or my preoccupation with it ebbs, I have lost my grip on chronology. I also forget things. I don't remember anything about my flight from the US; I remember only standing before a huge board in the airport, here, looking at hotel listings. After Fritz said good-bye, he hopped in a taxi. He stood at the edge of a busy road right in front of Parliament, where there were hundreds of taxis on the road, all with illuminated yellow bars of light on their rooftops, coming at us in a constant swarm, and Fritz stuck his hand out and one dropped out of the swarm and stopped right in front of him. Throughout the night, Fritz had been telling me that his party—he was a local councillor in a satellite city—was going to storm a general election in the spring, and wipe out inequality by raising taxes and putting unemployed people back to work, and that night, as I stood before the Parliament building, with its enormous white columns, I realized he had brought me there in part to show me the trophy he prized but also to suggest the pointlessness of being apolitical. The building is impressive. It's a wonder. During the day, tourists walk around it like the apes around the obelisk in *2001*, and you cannot blame them. That's the way I felt, staring up at it. But after a while you don't feel wonder. You start to feel panic, because you realize that human beings are possessed by the idea that they must fill the world with objects and ideas that will outlive them, and you suddenly glimpse the fires that burn below human despair. I think of Fritz fondly, and the fondness comes from an instantaneous nostalgia—the knowledge that I'll never see him again, not ever, and that he may not even remember meeting me, because every night he goes out drinking he finds somebody to proselytize to, to borrow cigarettes from, and to leave at the feet of the symbol of his hope for a transformed and just world.

Saskia and I have come to the outer ring road. It's eight lanes wide, four in each direction, plus lanes for buses and streetcars. An underground passage runs below it, and there's no way to cross it otherwise. There are posters up and down the white-tiled corridors for exhibitions, concerts, and films, and advertisements for magazines, perfumes, and tourist destinations. There is also, curiously, at the halfway mark as you cross beneath the street, a chrome panel in the wall that is tallying, in red digitized numbers, the population of the world. It makes a ticking noise. I feel, though I can't explain why, a desire to watch it—that last digit changes every half second, the second-last digit flips every five seconds. Saskia doesn't notice that I've stopped until I call after her and she comes back and stops and watches it with me for a while. She gives me a funny look. We stand there for maybe half a minute, and then it's unreal, the numbers become merely numbers, and I can keep moving.

I had an infection once that made me very sick, and I remember thinking I was going to die, and I didn't care. An infection? She nods. A rare one. I'd been in South America for a few weeks. I caught it from a bird. I'm glad you lived, I say. Me too, she says. Still, it's strange. You have terrible thoughts about life and death when you are that sick. I was in hospital for a month. Nobody could figure it out, until a specialist came in and said, Have you been in contact with exotic birds? I don't remember much from then—that was two or three years ago—but I remember the words *exotic birds*, because I saw nothing but blue and pink and orange and green feathers. I actually felt myself lying on them, and it was very soft, and I thought I had died. But then I said, Yes. And they all nodded. There was no medicine to take. They just kept me in a bed and watched me, and hoped I would live.

I was once really seasick, in the Sea of Japan, I say. We surfaced in a powerful storm, and I had been ill for a few days anyway, with I don't know what, and the only thing

I remember was needing to get off the boat and drown as soon as possible. She nods sympathetically, then she says, Janos thinks you are in the CIA. The CIA? Like a spy? Not like a spy, she says. He thinks you torture people. Good God, I say. Does he really think that? It would be perfect for him if you were in the CIA, she says. But does he seriously think that? She says, Who knows? We come to the escalator that will take us back to the surface. We stand to the right, and two kids run past us on the left. It took me about forty-eight hours after arriving in the city to realize that there was a system for standing and walking on escalators—stand on the right, walk on the left. That was a pretty confusing forty-eight hours. One guy kicked my ankles, and a lot of people shoved me. Now I feel like I ought to shove and kick tourists who don't understand the routine, not because I'm angry but because I think systems everybody understands are valuable, and I'd hate to see one collapse. We reach the surface, under a large shelter. It's not snowing anymore, but it feels colder. From here you can see how, to the north, the ring road rises high above the buildings. There are billboards all over the place, and some are digital and flashing. There are high-rise office buildings and hotels along it. Inside the loop, and built into the side of a small mountain, is a stadium. It's where they play soccer, and whenever there's a game between two particular teams from opposite sides of the city, the streets fill with speeding armored trucks and ringing sirens and blue flashing lights, and you see riot police all over the place. I had this explained to me one night. I was in a café and saw a bunch of police cars and a paddy wagon that resembled an APC barrel down the street, with flashing lights and loud sirens. I thought it must be something serious, but nobody around me even looked up. Beyond the stadium and the high-rises, about twenty miles away, is the airport. Over the past few weeks, the weather has shut the airport a few times, so people are taking trains to get outside the city now. I'm not in the CIA, I say to Saskia. She gives me a look that says it's not at all necessary to state the obvious. But I feel the desire to explain anyway, and say: I was on subs for most of my career, then got out of the Navy and tried to make some money. When that failed I joined the reserves, and as a reservist I went to Iraq. I worked with a team in Baghdad that provided intelligence to troops that were fighting, but my work was mostly done at a desk. Saskia asks me what I mean by intelligence, because, perhaps, the word has brought her thoughts back to the notion of spying and the CIA. Information, I say, just informa-tion. Tell me about life on a submarine, she says. What do you mean? I ask. What are the people like? Well, I say, there are two kinds of submarine people — there are the boomer people and there are the fast-attack people. Boomer? asks Saskia. Ballistic missile submarines, I say. Oh, says Saskia. Do I sound different saying words like that? I ask. You do, she says, gleefully. I continue: Generally the guys who appreciate boomer culture are older, or guys with families. The deployment is always ninety days. It's a steady life. The guys who like fast-attack culture are generally younger, and wouldn't care if they were deployed for ten years, so long as there was action. Only the best officers with the best records get on nuclear subs, and they're paid more than anyone else, and they train for longer. And that was you? asks Saskia. That was me, I say. So you're smart, she says. I was ambitious, I say. And that's why you have so much money, she says. The money isn't from the Navy, I say. And I say nothing else. The truth is that all the money I'd saved from my first stint in the Navy was wasted on a failed business. I got hazard pay for my reserve deployment in Baghdad, and with that money I started another business—an intelligence firm, of which I was the sole employee—that I brought to Baghdad as a civilian. And it's that business that made me a fortune. What's it like to be on a submarine? she asks. I pause to consider, gratefully, her sense of diplomacy—letting me off easily about Iraq by asking me about a thing she probably has no real interest in. How do you mean? I ask. Do they rock a lot? Oh, submarines rock quite a bit on the surface, but once you submerge, the rocking subsides the deeper you go. Eventually there is no rocking. It is all very still and quiet. The only time you remember you're underwater is when the ship angles to make depth changes.

That really is the truth—you forget you are under-water. You have jobs to do. You stay busy, and you stick to a schedule. You are aware of time only because your activities remind you what time it is. You realize that the farther you get from the outward and obvious signs that days and nights exist, that is, natural lightness and natural darkness, the more painstakingly you must celebrate the rituals of night and day. If you are eating pancakes in the mess deck, it's morning. If you're eating leftovers, it's midnight. You run drills. You relax when you're told to relax. You exercise. You have to exercise, or you will experience a strange exhaustion—an exhaustion of mind, in which you can neither think coherently nor sleep. You're on a six-hour duty watch every day, and for those six hours you are intensely focused on a small space in front of you. The working conditions you face in a sub are completely unique, and almost everybody who is not a sub-mariner would find these conditions deeply unpleasant. But if you can hack it for a little while, it all normalizes. It's a routine, and you look forward to the breaks you get from time to time, surfacing and looking up. If you are Officer of the Deck and you are in charge at night sometime, and you get to open the bridge access hatches, you might witness something pretty extraordinary—the clear night sky, full of stars, after weeks of being submerged. I was Officer of the Deck once on an Arctic transit. I drove the boat through the North Pole and cycled around it twice. We were there in wintertime, when there were only about four hours of daylight each day. We popped up in that daylight and got on the ice and had a snowball fight. For a reason I can't explain, it didn't feel very cold. A lot of the guys were out in T-shirts, shorts, and bare feet. They just ran and ran and ran. We had come through quite a few feet of solid ice, which the sub does easily, and we were on top of thousands of feet of empty, cold water. One of the things you hear a lot from young officers is the surprise they feel standing in front of the attack center, at being so young and being responsible for the launch of ballistic missiles, Tomahawks, and torpedoes. The message you get from senior officers from day one is to never forget that the submarine insignia, the dolphins you wear on the breast of your uniform, is a warfare qualification. You learn basic functions and damage control, but what it is really all about is learning how to employ the sub as a weapon. This is why no thirty-year-old officer ever stands in front of the command launch console and comments on how weird it is that he, just this ordinary nerd who somehow ended up in the Navy, is going to launch a cruise missile.

Saskia opens her mouth but says nothing, then closes it. Say it, I say. She says it's not a happy story — it's about her parents. I tell her it would be nice to hear. I don't believe you, she says. Well, I say, now it will be awkward if you don't. We continue, and after a considerable pause she says, When we moved away from this city, when I was a girl, we lived in Spain. My father was a civil engineer. We lived in a village full of men who looked like mushrooms. My mother was from here, but my father was from Spain. Leaving here made him happy, but it made her sad. How long did you live there? I ask. Ten years. About ten years. We left when my mother died. I was fifteen. Then we spent three years in Athens, and my father died, then I went to university in Brussels. Then I came here and got a job. Do you still have family here? I ask. Cousins, uncles, she says. It's tough to lose your parents so young, I say, which is, I think, the same thing I said when she first told me. She says yes but not sadly, just agreeing. My mother's death caused my father's death, she says. Her death took a long time. She became tired of toxic medicine — every time the doctors gave her something, they would joke that it would kill a horse, different doctors, always a horse — and she decided to die. My father saw every hour of his life as a series of decisions that led to her death, and became depressed for about a year — our first year in Athens. Then one morning he woke up and shaved his beard and put on a suit. I told him he looked happy. Happy? he said. No, but I'm not sad. Your mother decided to die instead of going on living with us in Spain. I'm not sure when I'll be back. Then for the next two years he drank and womanized and stole money from his own business, and got very fat. In the end he died because of high cholesterol. Did he give up working? I ask. No, he kept working. He designed sewers. One day I was at home and he had grown very fat and his eyes were turning yellow, and he said, The function of a civil engineer is in all cases to ease the flow of human misery. We remove barriers to human connectedness and progress. Because of us, man could create cities. He was gentle and optimistic all his life, she says. But he had no courage. She stops and looks behind her, because she has heard the dinging bell of a streetcar at a stop at the bottom of the street. My feet are getting cold, she says. How are yours? My feet are fine, I say, but I don't mind getting the streetcar. We wait. We watch the streetcar climb toward us. It has one bright light, a Cyclops eye, that points down at the street and makes the wet rails sparkle. Do you want to get some dinner tonight? she asks. Sure, I say, I owe you for today. Not at all. If it weren't for you, she says, I'd probably be sitting in that café with Janos, complaining about the capitalists.

The streetcar stops and we get on. It's crowded, and this disappoints Saskia, who had wanted to sit and rest. She holds on to a pole and I grab a dangling loop. At the top of this street, there's a palace in two parts, the upper and the lower, and a garden in between. In the upper palace, one of the most famous paintings in the world hangs. It costs a lot of money to get in, and all they have is that painting and five or six rooms of old artifacts. People go straight to the painting and leave. They walk right up to it, take video cameras out, and film it, and on the way out, they complain. I heard an English couple complain that it was not very good. An American man said he thought it would be bigger. Nobody pays any attention to the other stuff. One room has nothing but Mesopotamian artifacts—it claims to be one of the largest exhibitions of Mesopotamian art in Europe—and, on the two occasions I visited, I spent most of my time there. When I was in Iraq, with the Navy, Mesopotamian art and artifacts were being looted. And when I went back, as a civilian contractor, I met, and worked with, people who were trying to locate and rescue the pieces. One guy sat in my hotel room and sobbed. He'd been the curator of a museum, and everything had been taken. He came in smiling. We shook hands and he told me a joke. We had some tea. I never understood how Iraqis drank hot tea when it was 120 degrees, but I did it anyway. He'd gone to Cambridge, which meant he spoke better English than I did. He was discussing various pieces matter-of-factly, handing me folders. He showed me a database on his computer that listed each artifact, and the progress of the investigation into its whereabouts. Then he came upon one piece that was in no way different from the others, not at all special, not more valuable, not larger, and he started sobbing. He sobbed and sobbed, in that tiny room, with the curtains drawn, in the middle of summer.

Being here, and having no job to do, seemed about as far away as I could ever get from that moment. But then I walked into that room in the palace and found myself surrounded by Mesopotamian art, so I stayed awhile.

Do you mind me talking about that stuff? asks Saskia. Not at all, I say. Are your parents alive? she asks. Yes, I say. Were you ever married? No, I say. She seems satisfied, and she leans down to look out the windows and check where we are. The streetcar stops, and more people board, about six or seven, and push us closer together. They shake the cold out of themselves by hopping and clapping and rubbing their hands together. The road suddenly becomes steep, but the streetcar stays smooth and quiet. In the spring and summer, she says, we should have a picnic in the palace garden. Good idea, I say. I've walked through the garden a few times. I'm drawn to parks in winter. I sit on benches and watch the snow, or I enjoy the cold sunshine or the gray wind. I don't do anything. I just observe, and stay very still, until it's too cold to stay still. The parks and gardens are usually attached to a palace or an imperial office that makes me think of power and of glory and how these things, here, have passed into history like an artifact. In Qatar I sat in a room the size of a hangar, and on the walls were five hundred large screens flipping through live satellite and ground surveillance of every inch of soil in the various theaters of war that stretched from the Horn of Africa to eastern Pakistan. We had something smaller in Baghdad, in Camp Victory. I used to sit and watch and make notes and disseminate bits of intelligence, and then I'd go have a coffee with Italian commandos and intelligence officers. I met a bunch of French officers in Qatar, and found out the French military was taking part in small-scale but extremely violent combat with Iranian forces near the border. It was not official combat, but engagements took place. The Syrians and Iranians were fighting Americans. Israeli commandos were fighting Iranians. It was all happening. I led a four-man Forward Dissemination Element. Our job was providing surveillance, reconnaissance, and targeting intelligence to coalition air assets and ground forces. We worked with the 2nd Marine Expeditionary Force, the 3rd Infantry Division, and the 42nd Infantry Division. My days on rotation, which were long and busy, went like this: After a couple hours' sleep, I'd wake very early in the morning, grab a coffee, and head in to check SIPR for tasking. SIPR is the classified intranet system that, some months before I arrived in this city, a young guy named PFC Manning used to download hundreds of thousands of military documents and diplomatic cables, which he gave to WikiLeaks. Then I'd check ATO — air tasking orders. ATO is the flight schedule for war, published by the Combined Air Operations Center. It's a document that includes all scheduled flights and missions for all squadrons. After that, I'd check Air Mobility Com-

mand for theater transportation—C-130s shuttling between Qatar, Iraq, and Afghanistan. Then I'd check email.
These checks determined the battle rhythm for the day
and night. Outside the regimented nature of my FDE
work, Camp Victory was a place of incongruity and a stupefying lack of drama. In bright blue pools, Army guys
played water volleyball with the ugly hot Polish girls who
worked at the post exchange. Behind the palace, pacing
around alone and in a cloud of fathomless confusion,
General Ricardo Sanchez smoked cigars and scratched
his cheeks. Paul Bremer walked around with this practiced gaze of victory on his face, but in closed-link video
meetings he did nothing but scream and excoriate and
blame at the top of his lungs, or so I heard from people
who knew. From the bottom to the very top, the one thing
all American leaders had in common was an unpreparedness for the very thing they'd wake up to face the next
day. We drove around in SUVs, ate Pizza Hut and Subway,
drank Budweiser. We sunbathed. We surfed the Internet.
VIPs with entourages took tours around the camp. Bremer was trying to create a free-market epicenter at the
heart of the Islamic world, and Camp Victory was like the
epicenter of the epicenter. There was always the sound
of faraway firefights and detonations, and from time to
time we'd come under mortar attack. There was a lady
from Oklahoma working for KBR as a room-assignment
queen—a sixtysomething grandmotherly dyed blonde.

She probably made more money than half-decent basketball players in the NBA. She was responsible for all the hooches on our compound. One day my boss came in to get a room ten minutes before she was closing. He had traveled by C-130 from Qatar and was hot and tired. She was closing up early and wanted to go home. Come back tomorrow, she said. We said no, give us a room, but she did not. There were very nice Filipinos working for pennies doing our laundry. There was a guy working for a Dutch multinational that had the sewage and waste contract. He and I drank together often. I'd sometimes think of how absolutely perfect it seemed, to have picked this place, where the first cities appeared — Uruk, Nippur, Nineveh, and Babylon — where man invented civilization, to carry out a war, secretly fought by all the nations of the world, that would be the beginning of the final war, which would be waged for two hundred years, or five hundred, and fought all over the earth, and which would probably end with the total disappearance of one or two or three of the great cities on earth — London, Paris, New York — or perhaps all of them.

On my second stint in Iraq, as a civilian contractor, I set up IT networks and did a lot of investigation. In the end it was mainly computer surveillance, trying to evaluate patterns of chatter to predict insurgent activity, or locate insurgents behind the anonymity of the Web. I had a lot of nice equipment. It was always getting stolen, but it was insured, and I was making so much money that it didn't matter. I worked with various private military companies, engineering firms, the Iraqi police, and the US government. I made a thousand dollars an hour for a period of about four weeks, taking vast amounts of information across multiple systems and organizing them onto a database I built for the Army. The way I estimated my fees for the Army—I worked for the Army more than anybody else—was to dream up a figure that seemed unreal and add a zero. The Army didn't trust you if your fees weren't preposterous. I didn't spend anything. When I wasn't working, I sat in my room and smoked cigarettes, and I listened to the city. The hotel was quiet during the days. In the mornings and evenings, it was manic. Everybody had their TVs on loud. Phones rang. Voices passed outside my door. Many of the people on my floor were journalists. Some were long-term residents, like me, but most were short-term. As they walked by, equipment rattled off their bodies. Sometimes they came by in groups of two or three, whispering, or not whispering. They spoke many different languages.

After I returned from my private work in Iraq, I went back to my city in the desert again, the one I kept leaving and returning to, for the last time. I had money that seemed—at least for my way of living—unlimited. I rented a four-bedroom, three-bath place on half an acre of fine, green grass near a country club, about an hour

north of the city. I leased a gigantic black pickup — a Ford
F-250 — with leather seats. I was all alone, and I had no
furniture, just a couch and a TV, and some kitchen stuff.
I drove, once a week, to the nearest grocery megastore
and wheeled a shopping cart around the aisles slowly for
an hour or two, examining lots of things but buying very
few, and other than that I rarely left the neighborhood.
I mowed and watered the lawn a lot. I got to know a
guy who lived just down the road with his big family in a
six-bedroom, seven-bath house with a huge pool. Everyone in that development used a golf cart to get around —
mainly this was because it allowed them to legally drink
and drive — and my neighbor had a bright red one that
would do thirty-one miles an hour downhill. It had silver
spinning rims. A neurosurgeon down the road had a yellow cart, jacked up and gold rims. It could do twenty-
seven miles an hour. Mine was just white, and had no
speedometer. This guy, my neighbor, worked as a distrib-
utor entirely from home, and never wore anything but
shorts and T-shirts. He never had meetings. He never
had to go anywhere. He drove a large black Denali with
tinted windows and played old-school rap, like NWA, as
loud as possible. He had a few employees who worked
in an office, cold-calling, but he rarely saw them. There
was a time when distributors were linked to particular in-
dustries. If you needed something specific, you needed
a specific guy. If you needed steel, you needed a steel

guy. But my neighbor represented a new breed—guys who could get anything in a second, from bolts for submarines to tortilla-making machines to silicon chips to garden furniture to bricks to small arms to parts for Tomahawk missiles. He put the company in the name of his wife so he could classify it as a woman-owned business, which gave him priority for government contracts. I get an order, he'd say, for fifty thousand surgical coils. I go online and get a decent price from a guy I know who delivers quality stuff. Let's say each coil costs me fifteen cents. I charge my buyer thirty-five cents. That right there is nearly a motherfucking speedboat, he'd say, and by speedboat he only meant a secondhand, small motorboat with an ice chest near the driver's seat. I hear that, I might say. But that's small-time, he'd say. Big-time is military. I mark my prices up one thousand percent. My girl knows this. This girl he speaks of is his buyer in the Navy, who likes him because when he is on the phone with her, he turns into a right-wing hawk. This girl, he'd say, has to spend her budget, so she's just looking for a guy who will flirt with her and be patriotic. What the fuck do I care?

These conversations between him and me took place usually while drinking vodka on the rocks at lunchtime, poolside. We'd talk, his phone would ring, he'd bullshit for five minutes, pick a number out of thin air, and when they agreed, as they always did, he'd silently pump his fist, say good-bye, send an email to one of his employees with instructions, and say, to me, Speedboat, baby. He was a millionaire, I think, but he had so many outgoings that he barely scraped by from month to month. Eventually he got the speedboat, but his wife wouldn't let him take the kids out on it, and the neighborhood association wouldn't let him park it in his driveway, so he kept it in a storage facility thirty minutes away, visited it like a spouse in prison, and rarely spoke of it. He was a good guy, and he wanted to make money, have a nice life, raise his kids, have regular sex with his wife. And it seemed kind of insane to me that the very natural idea of wanting to be successful in order to create a comfortable life for your family had, here, taken such a bighearted, unassuming, funny guy and placed him in the heart of darkness.

The last time I saw him we were up late in his backyard. He'd been drinking vodka tonics through the afternoon and evening. I came over after dark, because I heard loud music playing on his outdoor speakers. The police came by a few times to tell him neighbors were complaining, and he turned the music down for a little while, but then a song he liked would come on, and he'd turn it back up. After midnight, his wife started coming out every ten minutes to tell him the kids could not sleep. I was wearing a jacket, and he was in swim shorts, bare feet, and a T-shirt. At around half past one, he started bouncing on his trampoline. He kept saying, Watch this, as though he was about to backflip, but all he did was bounce. Intermittently he delivered his philosophy on life as well as his philosophy on women. Finally his wife asked me to go home, so I left him there, bouncing on his trampoline, in the middle of the night, which was cool and starry. It was a few days later that I packed some things into a suitcase and got a taxi to the airport. I didn't say good-bye. I suspected that he knew me as the kind of man who came by and had drinks, not the kind of man who said good-bye.

I say to Saskia, What were we talking about? Picnics, she says. I was saying we should have a picnic in the spring. Sounds good, I say. My favorite thing to do in spring, she says, is to go to a park with a friend on Sunday morning with all the newspapers and spend five or six hours there and not say a word to each other, except to comment on the nice weather. And then we go for lunch somewhere outdoors and drink white-wine spritzers for a long time. Then we go back to the grass and look at the blue in the sky until we fall asleep. Good Lord, I say, that sounds nice. Do you do that often? She pauses and watches the street for a few moments. No, she says. I don't think I've ever done it, not like that. Everybody I know wants to talk. They read over your shoulder, and then they want to talk. Well, I say, I'm your man. She holds my elbow as though to thank me for saying something nice. If you get your apartment today, she says, tomorrow morning I'll come over with food and we'll have a breakfast that takes two hours to eat. I'll bring bread

and jam, and lots of butter. We'll have an egg each—
every course is small, and we eat them slowly. We'll have
mushrooms and sausages. We need buttermilk, meat, and
cheese. We'll get very smelly cheese. We need fruit. And
some newspapers. And lots of coffee. During breakfast,
we'll smoke lots of cigarettes, and when we're done we'll
open the windows and air the kitchen out. After that,
we'll play some music and look at the city guide. God,
I say, I hope I get the apartment. We could do it at my
place, she says, but somehow it doesn't feel the same. She
has a roommate. He's from Montenegro, and he works
and plays video games and spends a lot of time on the
phone to his mother. She looks up at me and her mood
has sunk a bit, because she is thinking that this is her life,
to share a small apartment with an adult who plays video
games, so she thinks of something comforting. At least he
pays his rent on time, she says.

The road levels out, and the streetcar accelerates. We
pass the palace and enter a large white square. All around
us is massive white imperial space. It really takes your
breath away—still, even though I've seen it many times
now. The inner ring is at the other end of the square, four
or five lanes in both directions, always swamped with
traffic. Two large avenues, one leading into the center and
one leading away, have curved in along either side of the
streetcar tracks. Cars are backed up on the avenue leading into the city, as far back as I can see. The avenue out

of the center is nearly empty, and the odd car flies by. Today, because it has snowed so heavily, there is almost nothing that is not white, except the red lights of cars that are ahead of us, and the black, gritted streets, and various flags flapping over hotel lobbies and on the tops of buildings. The lights in the hotel lobbies are red and gold. They look empty and extremely peaceful. We pass the first stop that is on the ring road, between a school for actors and a school for musicians, and Saskia tells me a little bit about them, that it is very difficult to get into these schools, and that the drama school is for teenagers but the music school is for children as young as six. If you are six, she says, and you have not been identified as a musical genius, it is probably too late for you.

Just before the next stop, as we are waiting at a traffic light, she leans down and sees someone, and starts knocking loudly on the glass. Manuela! she shouts. A girl in a big fur coat and big pink combat boots turns around. She's got dark red hair. Saskia waves. Manuela smiles and waves back. The streetcar starts to move again and they both point up the road — presumably to the next stop, where we will rendezvous. What a coincidence, I say. You'd think so, says Saskia, but I always run into people I know. You'll like Manuela. She's very pretty. I look back, and Manuela shrinks into the scrolling scenery. We stop and get off, and have to readjust to the cold — I put my hat on and she puts her gloves on, and we zip and button up again. Shall we wait or go to meet her? I ask. She's going in our direction, says Saskia, so we should wait. Yes, I say, but it feels odd to just wait here. Let's walk very slowly. Okay, says Saskia. We begin to walk back toward Manuela as slowly as possible. And she—I can see her now a long way off— is hurrying in our direction. I see that she is tall and thin. Saskia has mentioned Manuela to me before, and I have, I suppose, expected that she would be cool and stern, but I can already see that she is sort of goofy. She takes short, quick steps, with crossed arms. She holds her head down and looks up only when she nearly bumps into somebody. I know that Manuela used to work with Saskia and now works for the central bank. She's more interested in her work than Saskia is. She is always working late, writing papers for conferences, having power lunches. Saskia is happy to stay in research, working hard in rare bouts to write reports only five or six people will read in their entirety, and is always dreaming of new things to do outside of work. Saskia says that Manuela sometimes irritates her, because she has no interest in books or art or history, but then admits that without Manuela she'd have an uninteresting social life. There's a small park beside us, in which there is a statue of a huge seated figure—a poet. On the other side of the ring road is another figure—Saskia tells me this is a philosopher. They are real historical men, friends and rivals, who lived at the same time, about three hundred years ago—*aesthesis* versus *theoria*, Saskia says.

Manuela is close enough now to wave. Then she looks down again. Saskia stops, so I stop. There is no reason to keep walking. Manuela gets to us and is out of breath. She and Saskia talk for a bit, and I don't understand anything but hello and how are you, and the cold. Then Saskia says, We have to speak English. So Manuela switches to English. We're going to buy him a new coat, says Saskia. And then we're going to look at an apartment for him. An apartment! says Manuela. How exciting. Where? Saskia says the name of a street, or an area, I suppose. You must be rich, says Manuela, but not in the way Janos said it. You were in the Navy? she says. I nod. Saskia says, I've just learned he was on submarines. You don't look American, Manuela says. Sorry, I don't mean there's anything wrong with looking American.

It is agreed that Manuela will come with us. I am pleased and not pleased about this. She is, as Saskia said, very pretty, so I am as happy as anyone would be to walk around with her. But I have already met Janos and now Manuela, and I start to feel that I am meeting people I'll see again. It is not that I don't like them. It is simply that they reinforce the idea that you can never escape who you are, never truly anonymize yourself. Even if you never speak to anyone, people see you, and they get to know you for themselves. We cross the road through another underground passage. Manuela doesn't ask any more questions about the Navy, or about me at all, which is a relief, but she tells a funny story about an office colleague who went with her to a conference last week, and who is uncomfortably antisocial. She met some interesting people at a dinner event but he followed her around, reminding her they needed to go back to the hotel and sleep. Every interesting conversation that almost happened with these interesting people was ruined by the colleague, who introduced serious questions about economics whenever the opportunity arose. She went back to the hotel with him, then waited an hour and sneaked out. When she returned a few hours later, very drunk, there was a note that he had slid under the door, saying he was disappointed that she hadn't done as he said. He's not my boss! she says. If it weren't for people like him, says Saskia, economics would be left entirely to people like you. That's a terrible thing to say! says Manuela. Saskia rolls her eyes. I feel I understand exactly how this friendship works.

We stop in front of a large department store, which is all glass. Manuela suggests we keep going. This is where my colleagues get their suits, she says. You have to be careful or you will come out looking like a civil servant. Saskia says, He's just getting a coat. I say, Let's have a look here and go somewhere else if we have to. We walk through the entrance into a thick gust of heat. All the walls are mirrors and all the effects are chrome. The light is bright and the music is loud. It's electronic Muzak—

a bass line repeating with chiming and twinkling bits inserted. The sensation of walking into this environment out of a freezing, old city is profoundly unpleasant. I take off my hat and Saskia takes off her gloves and Manuela takes off her coat. She is wearing a little brown-and-green dress, and tights. Saskia has told me she is a man-eater, and this is easy to imagine. She ties her hair up in a ponytail. She has a small, slightly freckled nose and green eyes. Do you need anything? I ask Saskia. I'm broke until next week, she says. How about you? I ask Manuela. I'd never buy anything here, she says, for women at least. Okay, I say, and we go straight to the escalator. What kind of coat are you looking for? asks Manuela. Something better than what I have now, I say. Buy something trendy, she says. I say, I'm not a trendy person. I'm thinking of something classy, something I can wear until it falls apart. I see, she says, and looks at my boots. I pick a foot up so we can all examine the boots, and think about them in relation to a coat. I like my boots, I say. Me too, says Manuela, but they're combat boots. They don't look like combat boots unless you hold them up like that, says Saskia. I put my foot down. Oh well, I say. I can buy classy shoes another day, when it gets warmer.

We land on the second level, which is still the women's section, and Manuela, before we turn onto the next escalator, grabs a low-cut red dress with shoulder pads. See? she says. My mother would wear this. And suddenly something catches her attention, and she disappears across the floor and among the high racks of dresses and tops and sweaters and skirts and jeans. Saskia gives me a look. You okay? I ask. Fine, she says. She stresses you out? I ask. No, says Saskia. She's just Manuela. Saskia looks upward, to the next level. I am below her on the escalator, two steps behind. I am looking up at her body and the back of her hair. She takes her coat off and places it in the cradle of her crossed arms. The next level is divided into men's formal and casual, and there is hardly anyone shopping in the formal section, just some middle-aged men looking at suits. The casual coats have zippers on the sleeves or logos or writing on the back or they are made of shiny fabric. The larges are too small — the sleeves are too short and the shoulders are too narrow — and the extra larges are too big. They all make me look as though I want to look younger. But I don't feel younger. I feel my age. I feel, now that I am forty-one, that I was born forty-one, that this number was somehow encoded in my DNA — this number was mass-produced by every cell of my body my whole life and for most of my life powered my bewilderment with the way everybody else acted, or what they wanted, or how they went about getting it. As a joke, I try on a coat that is blue and pink and has three small white stripes in a circle around the biceps of each sleeve and Saskia waves me away from the section entirely. I follow her. There is a ledge from which we can stare down at the level below, and we see Manuela inspecting an unsightly coat that would, no doubt, look nice on her. Saskia sighs. She seems eager to get out of here. Perhaps because her father was a civil engineer who ate himself to death, she equates the efficiency and usefulness of contemporary commercial architecture with ruthlessness and disease. She likes old, small, run-down places. In her camera phone she has photos of a thousand crumbling doorways and rusted gates. Since I have known her, she has added dozens. She has photos of broken windows in palaces and overflowing trash cans outside official buildings.

I see a coat on a headless mannequin at the other end of the floor, in a row of headless mannequins wearing nice coats. The coat is gray, almost silver. We walk to it. We stand beside the window overlooking the street. The coat has a lapel collar and epaulet sleeves and hidden buttons. Saskia says, It's beautiful. She runs to find one my size. It's ninety-nine percent cashmere and one percent cotton. It's so soft, says Saskia. But look. She holds out the price tag, which is hanging out of the cuff. I don't make that in a month, she says. It really is nice, though, I say. Yes, the best by far, she says. If you can afford it, you should get it. I feel inside the sleeves. It is expensive, but it's also one of the nicest coats I've ever seen. And I may never buy a coat again. Put it on, says Saskia. I put my old coat on the ground and kick it away from me. I take the new coat and put my arms through the sleeves and pull the collar to my neck, and it fits. It's a lot warmer than my other coat. It falls to my knees and there's a large slit up the back.

Now Manuela appears. What do you think? I ask. Very stylish, she says. Is it expensive? A little bit, I say. A lot, says Saskia. Maybe, I say, but I don't plan to buy myself any more coats for a long time. My colleagues wear coats like this, says Manuela, but not as nice. Your colleagues do not wear this coat, says Saskia. That's what I said, says Manuela. Not as nice. Well, I say, it's pretty conservative. I'm not trying to stand out. That's what I mean, says Manuela. You won't stand out. I stretch my arms to make sure the sleeves are the right length, and they are perfect. I say, How about gloves and a scarf now? Let me pick the scarf, says Manuela. Okay, I say. You need some color, she says. What's wrong with gray? I ask. She looks at Saskia and says, Exactly. She departs, and Saskia says she will look for some gloves. Something heavy, I say. I go find a mirror and have a look at myself. It is strange to spend this kind of money on anything that does not move or can't be lived in. But this is not the beginning of ostentatious spending. This is just the once. Manuela returns with a scarf. I knew it the second I saw it, she says. It is a silk scarf with thin tassels at either end, light blue patterned with large, narrow-lined, orange-pink squares. What do you think? she asks. I love it, I say, but it doesn't look very warm. No, says Manuela, it doesn't, but you can't wear a big wool scarf with that coat. I put it around my neck. You're probably right, I say. Tie it, says Manuela. Okay, I say, and I make a knot and pull tight, which strangles me. I look at myself. Oh, I say, and untie the knot. Have you worn a scarf before? she asks. I don't think so, I say. The only coat I would have ever worn, before I arrived here and bought my ugly coat from the Arab, was a peacoat, and you do not need scarves with peacoats. Give it to me, she says. She makes a loop, which she wraps around her neck, and pulls the ends through the loop. She tugs it tight. The tassels dangle over the breast of her dress. See? she says. I see, I say. I take the scarf and tie it in the way she has demonstrated. Much better, she says.

Saskia returns with a few pairs of gloves. We all look them over. Manuela rubs them on her cheek. Then she sniffs them. Try these, she says, and hands me a pair of thick black leather gloves with brown fur lining. Manuela reads the label and says, Beaver, I think. Beaver? says Saskia. Now I'm wearing everything—the coat and the scarf and the gloves. And my boots. I look at myself in the mirror and feel different. Nobody changes himself from the inside. Nobody wills change from the innermost depths of his soul. This is because a person cannot ever look within himself, or search himself, or witness an emotion in himself. A person looks at a chair, and the chair becomes hatred. Or a lightbulb flickering in a bathroom. Or a doorway. Or a shelf full of books. Or a house. Or a city. Or a temperature. Or a kind of light in the sky.

Or an articulated thought, or a dream—which is where thoughts become externalized facts. Or a reflection of himself. You look at yourself in the mirror, and feel hatred. But you have not felt hatred. Hatred stares back at you. This is what hell will be. A room, without walls or dimension, full of all the objects that hate you. Not fire and cinder, not pain, but mundane views of streets, television sets, and acquaintances.

Some weeks ago, when it was sunny and clear, and not too windy, I took a long journey by train to the uplands just south of the city. It was a weekday, and the train was full of empty seats, and I flipped through a newspaper I couldn't read. The train blinked out of the suburbs. There were yellow and white houses with sharply angled rooftops sparkling with snow and ice. Smoke rose out of their chimneys and light flashed off their windows. When the houses were all gone and there was nothing but countryside, the train accelerated. There was nobody but me then—everyone else had disembarked at the suburban stations. I fell asleep. It was one of those sudden, accidental sleeps, which I had never been capable of until I arrived here. When I woke, the train had come to its terminus. I had missed my stop. The train was silent. The engine was off, and so were the heaters in the cars. There were no other trains in the station. I stayed seated for a few minutes. Since I have never felt so calm in my life—or have no memory of a time when I felt this kind of calm—sometimes I like to sit and dwell in it. It's like floating in the distant wake of a huge ship, a ship you no longer see, which has moved into fog. The open sea smells like nothing you know how to smell, and it makes no noise, though there is a great noise in it, deep beneath you, which carries you even though you cannot feel yourself moving.

Eventually I decided to get off the train and go for a walk. There was no point worrying about having missed my destination, since it was not an important destination. A girl at the tourist office—I had gone to the tourist office to get brochures in English on walking tours—had suggested I go there, a small and pretty village in the mountains, where the children in the city went to learn to ski. Now, as far as I could tell, I was on the other side of the mountains, in the flat and vacant sprawl of the bottom of a huge valley. The station was just two low-lying platforms, with narrow shelters and a hut at the end. There was a guy in an orange high-viz jumpsuit pulling a gas-powered generator on wheels behind him. He saw me get off, and he stopped what he was doing to watch me, amused but also infuriated. I didn't know what I had done wrong, but I gave him an apologetic smile. I walked the length of the platform, through a gate, and into the small town. There were cars parked on the streets, and the shops were open, but there was nobody walking around. Because of the extreme clarity in the sky and the bright sun near its noontime winter apex, the streets were — as I walked around them — alternately very warm in the light and freezing in shadows. Shadows stretched across empty lots; chimney smoke made shadows too. The shadows of delicate weathervane animals stretched monstrously over the streets. And when you walked from a patch of light into the shadow of a building or a house, your breath appeared. I had never seen anything quite like it, so sudden, so delineated. This was before I had my boots, so my feet quickly became cold and sore, and I wanted to sit. I found a hotel with a view, from its restaurant, of the motionless plains that lay to the southeast. The hotel was old and quaint and a little depressing, and the woman serving me spoke no English. A small fire burned, and I sat close to it.

After about an hour an American man came into the dining room. He had a laptop, a wireless modem, a mobile phone, and a sat phone. He found a table as far away as possible, but the restaurant wasn't large, and when he spoke on the phone he spoke as though he were shouting across the Atlantic. He talked about energy, and drilling, and also about sustainability and diversification. He was ex-military. Even if he hadn't looked ex-military, being in the military creates a way of speaking. I placed him from the South — North Carolina, maybe Tennessee, though it gets harder and harder to tell. After a few long conversations he closed his computer and put everything in his bag and leaned into his chair, really sank into it, and pulled his baseball cap down, the way a cowboy pulls his hat down to go to sleep, and crossed his arms, and he looked out the window, just as I had been doing. He was probably my age, maybe a little older. He had closely cropped gray hair. I considered it too strange that two American men had come all this way to stare out the same window, so I got up and started to leave. Nice view, he said. Sure is, I said, and kept walking.

I went back to the train station and checked the time for the next train back to the city. I couldn't make sense of the timetable. The man in the high-viz jacket was gone and there was nobody else around. I sat on the curb and smoked a cigarette. I figured another train would come along soon. I finished my cigarette and walked over to the hut to look for somebody, but it was padlocked. I went back outside the gate and started to light another cigarette when the American man drove up in a black Range Rover and rolled down the window. I could hear country music playing in the car. It was a weird thing to hear. You trying to get back? he said. Affirmative, I said—I wanted him to know that I knew he was military; I wanted him to know that he did not blend in. Army? he asked. Navy, I said. What the hell are you doing out here? he asked. I missed my stop on the train, I said, and I figured I'd have a look around. I'm just here visiting. He wore silver-framed, square sunglasses, and he mostly spoke to me while staring straight ahead, or into his rearview mirror. The next train isn't until the evening, he said. People come and go once a day. What's out here? I asked. A power plant, he said. A big motherfucking power plant. You live out here? I asked. Hell no, he said. I'm leaving tomorrow, back to the States. So, Army? I asked. Yeah, he said. Retired. Oh yeah, I said, me too. Forty-second infantry, he said. No shit, I said. I told him what I did, and that my FDE worked with the 42nd. Hey, he said, now that is some crazy-ass shit. Then he said, Listen, you got hours to kill, and I don't have shit to do. I've been wanting to drive out to some ruins since I got here. You want to join me? I looked up and down the deserted street. I thought of my cold feet. So I walked around the other side, opened the door, and climbed inside. The seats were of soft leather, and I had endless leg space. My God, I said, this is a sweet fucking vehicle. I was worried he might go on about Iraq, or talk about his work, or ask me a hundred questions, or pointlessly chat about weather, but instead he cranked up the country music and said, All right, and jammed the gas down and we were screaming through the desolate and icy countryside. He took out some Kodiak and filled his gums with it. Want some? he asked. But he pronounced it, 'awnt sum. Sure, I said. He handed me an old white polystyrene coffee cup, the kind you drink out of on construction sites while wearing hard hats, and we were spitting and sucking and I was starting to feel a bit fucked up and queasy. I couldn't believe he was driving fast when there were patches of ice and compacted snow everywhere, but I placed great trust in him immediately, and assumed he knew what he was doing. The tremendous white and yellow light was everywhere, and warm.

His name, this ex-Army guy, was Early. That's what he went by. It could have been a last name or a nickname, or it could have been a first name. Early said, I love the Oak Ridge Boys. And he did seem to love them. They made him want to drive fast and say nothing. But what I really love, he said, is playing the Oak Ridge Boys out here, driving this goddamn machine. That's what I'm going to miss. I'll be happy to get home. I go abroad for six months, then I'm home for six months and play golf and take the kids to swim practice. I love that shit. You've been all over? I asked. All over, he said. Oil in Nigeria, Venezuela. Renewables in China, Ireland, fucking *Antarctica* once. You believe that shit? Antarctica, I said, holy shit. And obviously the Gulf. And I blast the motherfucking Oak Ridge Boys wherever I go. For a moment I became entirely lost in the beauty and mystery of blasting the Oak Ridge Boys from some massive ATV with a hundred headlights driving at night around the South Pole—a Sno-Cat or a Mars Humvee screwing recklessly into the black force of an Antarctic blizzard. I'm only messing with you, he said. I don't have kids. And he turned the music down. This is actually on the motherfucking radio, he said, without the accent. Can you believe that? We drove for a little while longer in the quiet discomfort his joke had created. I didn't know what was the truth, and I guessed he liked it that way. He changed the radio to a classical station and we were listening to strange violin music. He said, the minute he heard it: Alban Berg, fucking genius. Then he told me a story—by way of explaining his sense of humor—about a time, maybe ten years ago, he had put on a hat and some ragged clothes and sunglasses and fake redneck teeth and hopped on a bicycle and rode around his neighborhood. He called his girlfriend, who was at home, on his cell phone—while he was riding the bike—and said he'd heard on the news that a man fitting his description had raped and murdered some women and was last seen in their neighborhood. He told her to go to the window and see if the man was there. She saw him—this figure he described, himself, exactly, down to the color of his shorts—and she became so frightened that she started sobbing and hyperventilating and trying to scream. He told her to calm down and get a gun. Then he knocked on the door and ran away, and she shot the door to pieces with his .357. He smiled after he told me that. That was pretty damn funny, he said. Well, I said, what did your girlfriend say when you told her it was you? How the hell would it still be funny if I told her? he said.

He saw a sign on the road and slowed down to read it. This is us, he said. And we turned right, onto a road that was narrower and more overgrown at its edges. This is the first time you've been here? I asked. Yep, he said. He was lying, but I didn't take the lie as an insult. He thought of himself, I guessed, as a kind of entertainer, a magician of human responses. What he wanted, perhaps, was for me to feel that this place was unscathed by his own memories, and we could experience it for the first time together. He had lied out of politeness, in a way. We stayed on the new road for about five kilometers—I was keeping close watch of the way we traveled, and the distance, in case I had to make it back on my own, in case this whole thing was an epic joke—then turned left onto an even narrower road, hardly wide enough to hold the Range Rover. Then there was a little blue-and-white sign with a *P* on it, for *parking*. Nothing else, at that moment, but the sign. Early slowed down and pointed. See it? he asked. I sat up high in my seat. Not really, I said. Okay, he said. He turned into the parking lot. There was nobody else there, not a single car, but there were spaces for five hundred cars and for dozens of tour buses. He parked roughly in the middle of the lot, which gave us an unnecessarily long distance to walk. And he had initially parked outside the lines, so he hopped back in and reparked. He tried a few times, but the Range Rover would not fit inside a space. When he got out he said, This ain't a fucking Fiat Punto. We walked together across the lot, then straight onto the grass, which was brittle and slippery with frost. I had to walk in short steps. There was a strong smell of silage, and faraway clanking noises that echoed in the limitless distances. Early, who had heavy boots, walked without difficulty. I veered onto a gravel footpath, where the walking was easier. Ahead and below I could see that the earth was depressed, and in that depression I could see little mounds of bricks. Standing just in front of the excavated area was a large wall with a bird's-eye illustration of the site. I stopped at it, and read some of the information about it in English—there were five or six different languages, including, oddly, Portuguese, unless I don't know my flags. Anything interesting? Early shouted over. But he didn't wait for the answer, and I felt it had been less a question than a good-natured reminder that there are two kinds of people in the world, the ones who go see the ruins first, and the ones who read about them first. The site was a Roman military outpost, and the only structures that remained, though ruined, were the walls of a small barracks. The Romans had come here around 5 BC, and these walls were from the century after that. Early—every time I say that name in my memory I see him riding that bicycle, in sunglasses, and wearing those teeth, and I feel both joy and uneasiness—had stepped over the ankle-high wire divider that visitors were not supposed to cross and was standing in the site, spitting tobacco juice. I joined him. No shit, he said, couple of guys like us, over here, standing *in this spot*. I know very little about Rome, I said. In the *Aeneid*, said Early, Virgil declares that Rome came out of the ashes of Troy. The half god Aeneas led his people to Italy. There he defeated Turnus, king of the Rutulians. Early then recited these lines: The giant Turnus, struck, falls to earth; his knees bend under him. All the Rutulians leap up with a groan, and the mountain slopes around re-echo; tall forests, far and near, return that voice. Early spoke this as a kind of country funeral prayer, looking up instead of down. Then he paused and coughed, and spat into his cup. And, well, he said, this is as far as they got in this direction. We looked out, across the plains, at nothing, at wind. I thanked him for bringing me along. You bet, he said. To-morrow, he said, all this will be a memory. I'll be on some United flight drinking Scotch and talking to some idiot from Boeing who wants to tell me about efficiency and some conference I ought to attend, because his keynote will be about the very challenges I face every day. I nodded. It was obvious to me that he'd been to that place often. The spot he stood in seemed precise. He did not move from it until we left. I walked around and examined some of the old walls. I got down on my knees and touched them. I put my hands in dirt and grass. Early just stood there, like a man who knew it well enough to just stand there. I never thought it was odd that he'd taken me to that place. Everybody I was meeting — I can't remember now if I met Early before I met Fritz, but they were not the only ones — was taking me to sacred places.

We drove back to the train station much more slowly than we had driven to the ruins, and this made me suspect that Early, the comedian, had grown sad. On the way I told him about something I'd seen on the rooftop of Saddam's palace, a little bit of graffiti, all alone, written in permanent marker. It read, *None of this is possible without Ireland.* I paused after I told him that, and waited. Early, I suppose, was waiting for me to finish, but that was all I had to say. I figure, I said, with you as a history buff, you might have some idea of what it was about. He shrugged. Probably just some third-generation dickhead, he said, trying to rub his cock over everything. He dropped me at the station. It was the middle of the afternoon, and the sun was blazing, without heat, just above the horizon. I knew Early was going back to the city for his flight the next day, but I was glad he dropped me at the station rather than offer to drive me all the way. The drive to the city would take two or three hours, and we didn't have two or three hours of conversation in us. We shook hands inside the Range Rover. Good-bye, I said. Good-bye, he said. And then I walked into the station and sat down on a bench and waited a few hours. A train arrived, and three people got off. They wore heavy black coats and walked cheerlessly. I boarded, having no idea where the train was headed, but having assumed, correctly, that trains from there went in only one direction, and a few hours later I was back in the restaurant of Hotel Rus, looking out at the street, smiling at Mrs. Pyz when she walked by, and eager to get some sleep.

We are on the street again, and in the cold, and I am admiring the feel of the cut of my new coat and the warmth of everything but the scarf, which is not warm at all. Saskia says, We have about an hour before we have to see the apartment. It will take about half an hour to get there, but it's a good thing to be early. Manuela says, Landlords are thieves and liars. Don't be surprised if someone else comes along to look at the place and tries to outbid you. They'll be the landlord's friend. I say, You get them where I'm from, too. The street is wet and the gutters have gray snow in them. The sidewalks have been pounded into slush by shoppers. The unlit Christmas decorations strung between the buildings—huge chandeliers, sleighs, angels—rock excessively, like they are bursting to be turned on. I cannot wait for night. I cannot wait to walk under Christmas lights. Everybody has bags in their hands. There are beggars every hundred yards. They are mostly Roma, mostly women, young, with tiny babies. All you can see of the babies is little faces. Most of them are asleep but some are awake. The young women weep as you approach. They find someone to make eye contact with and weep all over them. And then you pass without giving anything and they say, Please, please, please, please, please, please, please, please, please, until you are out of range. The other day I was sitting in a little café I sometimes spend time in, and on the pavement outside the window there was a little cluster of telephone boxes, all badly vandalized—since nobody in the world uses payphones anymore. A young Roma girl, maybe sixteen and very pretty, sat outside, and glanced up at me with a really clumsy seductiveness every few minutes. I'd seen her before in that spot, and in the subway station nearby. I was inside having one coffee after another, reading Virgil—which I'd found in an English-language bookshop—for the lines Early pointed out. They are at the very end, of course, but one cannot understand them out of context. The girl was on a cardboard mat, as she always was when begging outside the café, kneeling inside a dirty sleeping bag, and she wore a puffy coat. A young man came by every so often—on each occasion I'd seen the girl, I'd seen him too, drifting by at irregular intervals, watching her from a long way off—to collect money. They chatted coolly, like business partners, and when he would leave she would smile or laugh at whatever he had said in parting. Men seemed to give her a great deal of money, perhaps because she was so pretty. Older women knelt beside her, gave her a coffee, and spoke with her for a while—maybe they discussed her welfare, or her future, or fished for allegations of abuse—but for most of the time she was on that cardboard mat, she just sat and did nothing, interacted with no one, and stared into nothingness. I don't think she'd ever noticed me before, but on this occasion, as I sat there reading Virgil, she, for whatever reason, kept glancing at me as though we were at opposite ends of a nightclub. I checked behind me, to see that there was nobody else she was looking at. And though it was merely one of those thoughts that go through your mind so fast that you have no idea they have arrived until they are gone, I considered the feasibility of walking outside, telling her I'd pay her for sex, and doing all the terrible sexual things I've ever wanted to do to women in my life, things my instincts wish for but I do not, in a long afternoon. That is a thought that takes some time to articulate but no time to think. And just as I was about to order a fourth or fifth coffee the young man returned. He kicked her in the face and I saw her jaw break—perhaps it did not break, but it seemed to move momentarily off her face. She fell backward and her head slapped the concrete. There were screams in the café. There were screams on the street. The young man stood over her, clenching his fists, the way Ali stood over Liston. She got up somehow, but she was staggering. People in the café were standing now, and shouting through the glass. The boy grabbed the girl and held her up against the telephone box and struck her so hard that blood splattered in the air, and she fell heavily and unconsciously to the sidewalk. A man on the street, an elderly man, tried to grab the young man. The young man pushed him back. People rushed out of the café to the street. The pedestrians on the street gathered, and they stood around the man in a circle and shouted. The boy shouted back at the crowd, then he jogged off. Then the crowd, for the most part, dispersed, except for three or four people who knelt beside the girl and two people who knelt over the old man, who seemed to be in shock, and who was the only spectator who had actually dared to intervene. But everyone else in the place had at least stood in order to express their horror, and some had rushed outside. I had stayed seated. I had never moved. I'd finished my coffee while he beat her. And it occurs to me only now, because until now I had isolated those memories from each other, that it was just an hour after this incident that I met Saskia for the first time, at the National Gallery. And now I remember the painting I was sitting in front of, while reading Virgil, when she approached and asked if I minded if she sat down beside me.

I had found a bench in front of the painting—a very small painting—which I found peculiar but not particularly exhilarating, and there was nobody else about at the time. I was spending lots of time in museums, especially art museums, and one of the things I gradually became more and more aware of was a ludicrous but entirely spooky sense, which presumably no one else shared, that human beings are unwanted disturbances, that the various works hanging nakedly on walls, for instance, are desperate to evict the living, because to have to watch us plodding around them is torture, and that day it occurred to me that the same could be said for the *Aeneid*, doomed for eternity to be read by students, snobs, and imbeciles. The painting was Piero's *Flagellation*. In it, three men are gathered in the foreground, on the right side of the painting, and they are staring in different directions. To the left of them, in the background, Christ is being whipped. I read, on a plaque beside the small painting, a little bit about the use of common perspective, which Piero introduced with his treatise, *Perspective in Painting*. Piero had been known principally as a mathematician in his time, but now he was known mainly for his art — and this painting, the *Flagellation*, had been called the greatest small painting in history. After reading this, I sat down and flipped through Virgil, and a little while later Saskia sat down beside me, putting a briefcase between us. She studied the painting for about ten minutes, then ate a sandwich. Since there is a rule prohibiting food, she ate it by looking around, taking it out of the briefcase, biting into it, and placing it back into the briefcase. I found this really amusing and smiled at her. She said, I recently finished the *Aeneid*. Well, last year. It's good, I said. I expected it to be very hard to read, but it's easy. A little while later, when we were discussing the Piero, which was to return shortly to its home in a museum in Urbino — it's probably already back there — she said that the major shift from Medieval to Renaissance art was the fact that the people in paintings were no longer representations of characters in narratives outside the painting but characters within a narrative. This meant ideas became embodied. Perspective, she said, was a crucial part of this transformation, because, among many other things, it forced the human eye to consider its subject first as a thing and less as a symbol. Before she left to return to work, and against my intention to avoid getting to know new people, we exchanged numbers. After she left I spent some more time with the Piero, as she suggested, since I had not understood what made it the greatest small painting in history, and found something really wonderful and mysterious in it, which I had entirely missed at first. After that, I went to the museum's bookshop, which was vast, and included, at one end, a spacious and tidy Internet café, and read a bit about perspective. It was unthinkably strange that something so obvious would have eluded art for so long. And when the question of it did arise, I read, a full, intricate understanding of perspective was achieved not overnight, as I would have guessed, but over a period of four hundred years. I had been born at a time when an understanding of optics was taken for granted, and when realism in art had already been born, perfected, and exhausted. It was disconcerting to think that if I had been born in the fifteenth century, or the sixteenth, I would have been incapable of understanding the physics behind artistic perspective. In the earliest art, such as Egyptian art, I read, works were constructed with vertical perspective. If someone were in front of somebody else, the artist simply placed the closer person below the person farther away. Often an object's position on the page had to do with its thematic importance to the story the painting was telling, so that you might have minor scenes playing out at the bottom of paintings, such as a battle, with small figures, and large figures above them. At this time it was not understood that the nearness and distance of objects could be represented by size, and the first evidence that artists had begun to associate size with depth in a field didn't emerge until late antiquity. Then, suddenly, from the early Middle Ages onward, interest in perspective vanished, and it would not re-emerge until the rule of Charlemagne and the Carolingian Renaissance. Throughout its history, at least until it became untenable as a method of inquiry, the study of perspective seemed to be, among other things, a sign that human beings believed in an intellectual destiny that was contained in the intersecting lines of reality; by studying those lines we studied that destiny. In Byzantine art, where principles of perspective were well understood, reverse perspective was often used, so that the farther away an object got, the larger it became. In this way, the vanishing point became the viewer, and, so the book I read speculated, the lines of convergence, which would have, in reverse perspective, naturally come from everywhere, represented the omnipresence of God. The breakthroughs that would take place in fifteenth-century Florence were driven by a handful of artists, all of whom were deeply influenced by each other and some of whom were profoundly influenced by the eleventh-century work of a man named al-Hasan Ibn al-Haytham, or Alhazen, who was born in the city of Basra, and composed his great work, the *Book of Optics*, while under house arrest in Cairo. Alhazen's discoveries resolved the ancient dispute between the mathematicians, like Ptolemy and Euclid, and the physicists, like Aristotle, over the nature of vision and light. He also showed that vision is not merely a phenomenon of pure sensation but also of judgment, imagination, and memory. In the *Flagellation*, the section of ceiling above Christ is filled with light. The light is miraculous: It has no source. Everything apart from that light is geometrically and optically explicable. Christ is aware of the light, but his torturers are not.

It seems like a long time ago that I read those things about perspective. Everything I have experienced here — even our bus ride into town this morning — feels like it happened years ago. Saskia and I once had a conversation about this time distortion. We were sitting in a café that is on the top floor of the museum of contemporary art. I had spent the afternoon there, and she came after work. She was in black pants and an ultramarine top with a fat

bow around the neck. She'd had a long weekend of parties, and looked exhausted. Our surroundings, she said,
so long as we keep them familiar, remind us of yesterday
more than, for instance, fifteen years ago, because, if our
whole life is in every memory, it is the recent memories
that seem more superficially consistent with reality. Go
somewhere you haven't been for fifteen years. Walk
around the places you knew, and try to think of what you
cared about the day before you got there. I did this recently, she said. I was sent away for work. I hired a car
and drove to the place I used to live. I had a sandwich
near a fountain I used to sit beside, and where I imagined
what my life would be like once I became an artist. I was
going to build a sculpture the size of a cathedral. I sat
at this fountain, and had a bottle of water and watched
people go by, and nobody recognized me and I didn't recognize them. My memory of the fountain did not seem
at all like a memory. It seemed like I had only had the
thought about being an artist that morning, and the reason I had flown there, for work—all that seemed like
something I'd done thirty years ago. And I'm not even
thirty. She turned her palms upward, then pulled her hair
back over her shoulders. A waiter came by and asked if
we wanted anything else. She ordered a cocktail and I ordered a sparkling water. I asked her, Are you disappointed
that you did not become an artist? Not at all, she said.
And only today do I realize that she meant Spain—some

fountain in Spain — and that she was, even if she did not know it then, telling me about her mother.

At every large intersection there are glass-and-metal entrances to the subway, and the unstable serenity of the crowds moving in both directions seizes suddenly at the mouths of these structures. We could take any of them, Saskia says, but maybe we don't want to squeeze ourselves into the same trains all these people are boarding. Manuela says, Let's take a taxi instead. This seems like a good idea, but the taxis are all stuck in traffic, so we keep going. The street curves and descends a bit, and we enter a square. I've been here several times before, but I've come from different directions. In the middle of the square there's an elevated section for pedestrians and picnics, with benches, and in the middle of that there is a tall pole with a large four-faced clock on top. There is a museum of engine-making, which is covered in scaffolding. All the buildings to the left of the scaffolding are bright white, and all those to the right are sooty. The work moves slowly. Since I've arrived, not a single scaffold in the city has moved, including the one in this square, which I have come across several times. The freshly blasted stone transports you back three hundred years, and makes you think of streets full of horseshit and buckets of human excrement and the knocking sound of carriages, and, though I am of course mixing things up badly, boy pickpockets and a villain with a dog. Saskia's phone buzzes in her bag. She lifts it out and checks it. It is either a long message, or she's reading it many times. Her face changes. Janos, she says. What does he want? asks Manuela. Nothing. She types something back, sighs, and stuffs the phone back in her bag. She looks around. You know what? she says. I think we're not early anymore. I'm not even sure if we're on time. How did that happen? I ask. I have no idea, she says. It took us twenty minutes to get here, and I thought it would take five. That's because I walk slowly, I say. You *do*, says Manuela. Let's hurry, says Saskia. She points to a little entranceway in the side of a building on the far end of the square, with a blue *U* outside it. We walk with quick steps across the middle of the square, across the raised platform, which has been swept clear of snow, though a thin layer has fallen since. This is the first time I've really hurried since I got here. Sometimes I walk fast to make myself look like a local, and I mutter things when people hold me up. I do this not out of dislike for tourists but out of love for the city. The city has, on certain streets, a tempo, and it's important to move in step with it. But I am not really hurrying, because once I get past them, and walk a little farther, I stop at a street corner and smoke a cigarette. Today I am actually hurrying. I feel exhilaration and fatigue. Here comes, perhaps, the end of a life. Forty-one years of waste. Or worse. The seconds are counting down in rapid red digits. We speed down the steps.

Some of the bigger stations are like miniature cities, but this one is just a large landing, a half-shuttered window to an unmanned ticket counter, and two escalators, one going up and the other down, and between them a stairway. We hurry down the escalator. Even though it's a long way down, you know if a train is there or not, and now there is no train, so we slow down. The platform is a gray slab dotted with pillars, purple and pearly. The tiles are small and square, like the tiles you find in showers. The benches are chrome. The ceiling is the color of coal, and so are the tunnels on either side of the platform. The monitor says our train is going to arrive in two minutes, and I can already hear it. Trains come every nine minutes on weekends and every six minutes on weekdays, no matter what time of day, except perhaps for very late, and in rush hour they are always full. You have to push your way on and throw yourself off. Nobody shows you any generosity, nor forgiveness. I do not travel at these times, but I sometimes stand in stations and watch. Now our train has arrived. It's a green train, and it's lit orange. It's not too crowded. Saskia grabs the latch, pulls sharply, and the doors open automatically the rest of the way. We step in. Saskia and Manuela sit beside each other, facing two empty seats. I stand and look up at the chart that plots the courses of the various subway lines. One day, when I feel I know the inner city well enough, I shall begin a slow exploration of the rest of the city by subway stops, and it may take a few years or it may take my whole life, or it may not even be possible, since I am not going to rush. I'm going to take the subway to each and every station, walk up to the surface, find a place to have a coffee, talk to somebody behind a counter for a while, ask them how they are, stroll around, find something odd, and go back home.

How many stops do we have? I ask Saskia. Four, she says. Manuela says something to Saskia. Saskia responds. They have momentarily abandoned English, and I feel guilty for forgetting that they'd been speaking English since we met. It cannot be easy, so I give them some time alone. Every once in a while there is a bright electric spark that lights up the tunnel, but apart from that, all you see in the window is your own reflection. My reflection looks at me with equanimity, but that equanimity is not in me. Saskia and Manuela are trying to figure something out. There's a disagreement, but it's not heated. Finally Saskia nods, and snaps her fingers. The train slows down. I sit. Saskia says, Manuela knows a better way, but we must go an extra stop. Are we going to be on time? I ask. Maybe five minutes late, she says. Manuela is reading a financial paper that someone left behind on a seat. It's orange-pink, like the *Financial Times*, and it's one I'd regularly buy and sit down with at my little café and imperfectly translate with the Italian waiter. Saskia tells her not to depress herself. The economy, here, like everywhere else, is in bad shape. Every time I read a gloomy prognosis in the paper, I feel a little thrill, Saskia says. It's shameful, really, she adds. Everyone's like that, said Manuela. Everyone feels a thrill when they see disaster in the news. Manuela looks at me. Don't you? she asks. I suppose, I say. Manuela goes back to reading her paper, and Saskia looks over her shoulder. She says, I hate the rich. Manuela gives her a quizzical look. I find that I suddenly don't know what to do with my hands. I say, because I feel a nervous need to change the subject slightly, that I remember an interview with a woman in Thailand after the 2006 tsunami. The reporter—this was, I think, BBC World or CNN; it was playing in a hotel room—sat down with the woman on some steps outside her house, which had been demolished, and they spoke about the woman's daughter. The woman told the reporter she'd held tightly on to her daughter, who was eight, until the force of the water was too great and she lost her grip. She hoped the daughter was alive, she said. She held up a photograph of the daughter, and instantly they cut to another story. I was half sickened by the way the story had been presented not as a piece of news but as a confession, not so that we would learn about the suffering taking place in Thailand, but in order that we might hate and then decide to forgive a woman who couldn't save her daughter, who let her daughter go, probably to save herself from drowning, a decision that was for her no more deliberate than the decision to breathe. But of all the things that disturbed me, what disturbed me most was the daughter's photograph, which had been presented very much, I felt, in the manner of a photograph of a lost dog you find stapled to telephone poles, as though the story were not at all the prostitution of human suffering but a public service announcement. Saskia says, I read, once, about a woman who lived in a flat with three children. For no apparent reason, she began to throw her children out the window, a five-story drop. First she threw the baby, then the toddler, then a six-year-old boy. The baby and toddler died on impact, but the older boy lived for a few minutes. Then the mother threw herself off and died. The older boy, while lying on the ground and dying, was interviewed by three journalists. Is that true? I ask. It is, says Saskia, except that it's an old story.

The walls of the tunnel go bright suddenly. We whoosh into the open air, the city. It is snowing again, or maybe snow is blowing off rooftops. Everywhere, there are gleaming red and white and orange billboards. There are high-rise hotels and office blocks of green glass and blue glass. Behind the billboards and the high-rises lies the stone maze of buildings stretching back for crowded miles. Manuela asks what Saskia and I have planned for later. Dinner, I think, I say. Yes, says Saskia, definitely, if you'd like. We have to eat, I say. Saskia looks at Manuela, pauses, considers whether to speak, then speaks: Do you want to join us? Manuela says, I'm going to dinner at Anton's. Oh yeah, says Saskia, I forgot about that. Manuela says, You should come. I hate Anton's dinner parties, says Saskia. Manuela crosses and uncrosses her arms, a gesture I interpret as a sign that she hates them too. The train is slowing down. We're coming to the stop for the city park. It's one of the biggest parks in Europe, right in the middle of the city. Manuela tells us that afterward they're all going to Chambinsky, a bar that used to be an old theater. Oh yeah? I say. Saskia says, It's huge. Sometimes they have live music on the old stage. They have lots and lots of billiard tables. Anton and Janos think they are professionals. They take themselves very seriously. Could you beat them? I don't know, I say, it depends on how good they are. I haven't played for a long time. Saskia and Manuela take a break from English to share a joke, which I presume is at the expense of Anton and Janos. Then Manuela says, Please, please come and beat them.

My father played a lot of pool, and he was very good. In fact, he was a three-cushion billiards champion. Three-cushion or carom billiards is, at least everywhere I know of in America, so unknown by ordinary pool players that it might as well be obsolete. You have a cue ball and two object balls. To score a point you must hit both object balls and at least three cushions with the cue ball; at least one of the object balls may be hit only after the cue ball has hit the cushions. It is a difficult game to play, and if you score a point once for every time you miss, then you can quit your job and play the game for the rest of your life. The average pool player who takes himself seriously—even guys who can run tables, on the rare occasion, in eight-ball and nine-ball—could play for an hour straight and never score a single point, except accidentally. A person who plays carom billiards always plays pool differently than a person who has never, or rarely, played carom billiards, and this is because a carom billiards player has a different concept of the ballistic space of a pool table. The rails are not something to avoid or use in emergencies; they are theoretical extensions of space. When I was a teenager, my father used to play me in eight-ball. To keep it close, he required himself to hit two cushions with the cue ball before potting a ball. Other times he played one-handed, or with a bottle of beer on his head. I practiced a lot, and though I was never as good as my father, not even close, eventually he had to stop hitting cushions, stop playing one-handed, and stop balancing things on his head. A good billiards player—and even a very good pool player—has an affinity for, or perhaps a natural understanding of, ballistics—internal, transition, exterior, and terminal ballistics. I used to say this to people I played pool with, and they looked at me the way you'd look at a person who says something very obvious while believing it to be profound. And yet none of them could appreciate the irony of the fact that the guy who won a straight pool tournament in Camp Victory, a nerdy Air Force guy who beat me in the semifinals of that tournament, was killed by a mortar while on the can a few days after his big win. The mortar had cleared the high Alaska walls and dropped squarely on him.

The train stops at the city park station. A woman with a stroller and a sleeping baby gets off, and the cold comes through the car and right through my nose and into my brain. I say to Saskia and Manuela, I wish those doors would close. They don't seem too bothered by it. Then there is some beeping and the doors begin to close, and I hear a shout. A man, running from the stairwell, making huge white clouds of breath around his head, is waving at the train, telling it to wait. He's wearing a black trench coat and a black winter hat. He seems like an unstable fissure in the fabric of reality, a wild blackness, expanding in the way that paper burns if you light a piece of it in the middle, and through which, if it reached us, the whole weight of time in the universe would crash in upon us, and burn and pulverize us, and the powder that remained would drift slowly into the stars. The doors close almost as soon as he jumps from the stairs to the platform, but he keeps running anyway. He runs straight to our car, straight at us, and slaps his hand on the window by the seats in front of us, where nobody is sitting. What's he running for? I ask. Maybe he's being chased by a tiger, Saskia says. Manuela gives Saskia a funny look. From the zoo in the park, Saskia clarifies. The train pulls away, and we pass by the man, who has already turned to find a seat to wait nine minutes for the next one. And the mystery of his hurry goes with him, silently, with the steam that comes off his head when he takes off his hat.

I've visited the park a few times. It's not possible to experience it in a single day. It's vast and variegated, with wide-open spaces and straight pathways, and secluded spaces with winding pathways. There are hothouses, rose gardens, a zoo, an amphitheater, a natural history museum, some ruins, the American and British and French ambassadors' residences. There's a large hill where you can get a nice view of the city and the surrounding lowlands. There are tandem bikes to rent, and bikes with trailers for small children. There are fields for sports, soccer and volleyball, basketball courts, a field for throwing javelins and discuses. And on and on. But in winter, as I have seen it, it's empty. Saskia tells me joggers flood the park in the mornings, but by the time I get there almost everyone has gone. It's just snow and ice. The ponds are frozen. The fountains are emptied. The trees are leafless. Large parts of the zoo are shut down, and hardly anybody visits. It feels good to come here after a few days of immediacy and noise in the city. Manuela says, I think you should definitely come to Chambinsky. Maybe so, says Saskia. They look at me. I can't think reasonably about anything beyond the apartment. Sure, I say, sounds fun.

Even though it does not sound like fun. The train starts to rise from the depths of the walled trench, to the level of the surface, then higher, above the first-floor windows, and higher still, above the rooftops, so high that you feel a dreamlike disconnection from the city, which appears, to one side of us, as a silver-gray and irregularly blinking boundlessness under a snowy, fogged, silver-gray sky. There isn't much light left in the day. Pretty soon, street by street, in dusk, the Christmas lights will switch on. When I first arrived, they were just beginning to string the lights up. Huts came out where the Christmas markets would be, but they were all padlocked shut. On the first day of Advent, in the evening, the lights came on and the markets opened, and instead of hurrying home to escape the cold, people began to hang around for a few more hours, in the markets. The nights attained a state of extreme slow motion.

When we get to our stop, Saskia stands first, then Manuela, then me. This could be your stop forever, says Saskia, jokingly, but that word, *forever*, suddenly has the same effect as that man in black running at us. I ask her, Do you have all the documents? She pats her bag. Do you have the money? she asks. I sure do, I say. We'll be a few minutes late, she says, but it's nothing to worry about. Half my mind is worried we'll miss the appointment, and half my mind is hoping we will. Half my mind has concluded that if I do not get this apartment, which I have never seen and which may be awful, it will be a failure so significant that I will have to pack my bags and go back to the desert. And half my mind is calm, telling me it doesn't matter, that there are other apartments, that hotel life is better anyway. I slap my gloves together. This, I guess, is nervousness. I put my hat on. Here we go, my mind says. The last time it said that was upon my second arrival in Baghdad, my arrival as a civilian. We were corkscrewing in on a jet that had departed out of Amman, and the city, as the plane angled down and back for turns, rose and crashed out of sight like waves in heavy seas might look to someone who has fallen overboard. I set my watch one hour forward, to Baghdad time. Then I said, Here we go. A person says a thing like that when, I suppose, he's decided to throw himself at the feet of the gods, without enough preparation, or when sufficient preparation is impossible. Saskia and Manuela put their hats and gloves on. The doors open and we walk down the platform. The station is elevated, and though we are in the middle of things, the height gives a false impression of remoteness. The station too—which is just a green hut leading to a staircase—gives that impression. On days I know I'm going to use a lot of public transportation—three trips or more—I get a day pass. Once the day pass is validated, you just hop on and off anything you like, as often as you like, and travel as far as you like. It works on buses, streetcars, trains, regional trains. You travel without impediments, and everything runs on time. I tried to tell Saskia once how impressed I was by the system. The system? she said. How could you live in a city without such a system? Exactly, I said. Why don't you buy a monthly pass? she asked. I get too much joy out of buying the daily pass, I said. The walls in the little hut are green and white, and there are two huge maps of the city: a transit map, with perfectly vertical, horizontal, and diagonal lines, and a street map. Saskia stops at the street map to point to the location of the apartment. She wants to show us how close it is. Manuela says, I have a map on my phone. I see a small empty rectangle beside the spot Saskia points to. A park. A park, I say. A park! says Saskia. We take the stairs down to the street and walk through an arched stone gateway to a hectic little transport hub, with bus stops and streetcar stops. A streetcar halts right in front of us, and a handful of people get off. A few dash across the road to the staircase that takes you back up to the subway station. The green pedestrian light — a green man — becomes a red man just as they get to the street, but this does not deter them. They have already decided to cross, so they cross. They hold their hands up to the waiting cars as if to say thank you for waiting. The cars behind those cars honk their horns. Everyone crosses, and the cars move forward. We are underneath the wide, elevated tracks, from which very large icicles hang. Another train comes in the opposite direction and the tracks make a thundering noise, and the icicles shiver. I imagine what happens when a thaw comes, when drops of water fall steadily and with great weight, and the icicles detach and plummet, and shatter on the street.

Manuela and Saskia walk as though they live around the corner, with assurance, a youthful at-homeness, without glancing at street names or numbers. We pass a halal butcher's, an African clothing store, a knockoff electronics store, a pizza place, and a shoe store with leopard- and zebra-patterned men's dress shoes. Then we turn down a smaller street. There's a hemp store and a store for bags and suitcases, a hairdresser's with a gaudy purple façade, then nothing but doors and numbers on doors, and unadorned postwar buildings. The sidewalks are snowy and icy. The cars are all snowbound, and there's trash beside the tires, and mounds of cigarette butts. This seems pretty depressing, I say, and for the first time all day I consider the possibility that I might dislike the apartment. I am not interested in postwar utility, pressed wood, and vinyl or laminate wood flooring. I am not interested in plastic toilet seats. Saskia says, Trust me, this is not your area. These apartments go for half your rent. Much less, says Manuela. Much less, Saskia agrees. We walk a few more minutes, then we come to another big intersection. The buildings on it are old and tall, and the ground floors are flower shops, cafés, a place to buy Apple computers, and a chocolatier. There are strollers being pushed by young, beautiful women. Now the street is full of old, sincere, beautiful buildings, with big stairways leading up to the front doors. The sidewalks have been swept clean, and are dry. We see a man pick his dog's shit out of the snow between two snowbound Mercedes, wrap it in a bag, and put that bag in another bag that is slung over his shoulder. In the basement level of a place we walk by, there's a single lantern hanging over some steps down to a little bar. The bar's name, says Saskia, translates as The Lantern. It's your local bar, says Manuela, whether you like it or not. The glass on the windows is stained amber, so you can't see inside. There's a blackboard outside that reads 13.00–02.00. It looks pretty serious and dull, a place Mr. and Mrs. Pyz might run. I imagine it's a nice place to have a late drink, a place you can talk to the bartender about the history of the neighborhood. And when two a.m. rolls around the bartender is happy to let you stay a while longer.

Ahead, there's a woman in a gleaming white wool coat and black tights and high heels standing on the corner of a T-intersection, smoking a cigarette and looking at her phone. We see each other from a long way off. She lifts her head. She has a long nose and dark eyebrows. This is it, Saskia says. The woman looks at us, realizes we are probably the people she's waiting for, smiles, then returns to her phone. I have a look around. There's a little store on the corner opposite, where, on mornings when there isn't anything in the place to eat, I might buy milk and eggs and ham and cheese and bread and sugar and coffee. Beside it is an awkwardly large flower shop, and this strikes me as strange until I comprehend the full view of what's in front of me, across the intersection. The rectangle I thought was a park when Saskia pointed to it on the map is not a park. It is a cemetery. The woman looks up again, and Saskia waves hello to her. The woman gives us a brief and businesslike smile and puts her phone in her bag. Her hair is brown and straight, shoulder-length, with a fringe. She's probably thirty-five. Her coat is opened at the front, and she's wearing a black dress. I feel the need to take off my hat and my gloves. It's painfully cold, but necessary, somehow. The woman doesn't seem cold at all. Saskia shakes her hand and introduces me, and then I shake hands with her. Hello, I say. Hello, she says. Shall we speak English? Yes, I say, I am sorry about that. Fine, she says. She does not wait to be introduced to Manuela. She says, Shall we have a look? She extends her arm toward the steps to the door, a large wooden door with an arched transom window above it. The building is tall and gray, and covered in dead ivy. Each window facing the street, on every floor, has a tiny balcony, enclosed by iron railings, not quite large enough to stand comfortably in but big enough for flowerpots. Please, I say, and extend my arm back to the woman. She goes up the steps and digs through her bag for keys. Her phone rings and she answers it while unlocking the door. Saskia says, It's on the top floor. Manuela says, with a sympathetic grimace, You'll have a nice view of the graveyard.

A friend once told me that the only time you ever really see a place is the first time and last time you're there — the day you move in and the day you move out. She wrote it in a letter, and sent it to me just days before I was commissioned. She had a rare and degenerative autoimmune disease and did not expect to live through the year. Her letter, which was over thirty pages long, handwritten, in cursive, began matter-of-factly. She caught me up on how she had left for college in New York, but became sick within a few weeks, then got diagnosed with this thing, which was serious, and had to come home. She was disappointed. I thought that was odd and heartbreaking — that, even when writing me the letter, when there was very little time left, she was still disappointed she had not attended college, as though knowledge were something she could pack in a suitcase and take with her, and might do her some good. I don't remember all of it, of course, but I remember it was a witty and positive letter, and because of that it was all the more painful to imagine a world in which she no longer existed. But that was an odd conclusion to leap to, since it had been years since I'd spoken with her, and, apart from one very strange day, I had not often thought about her since. Her name was Josephina.

When she was sixteen, the last time I saw her, she

was pretty, black-eyed, and of average height. She ran cross-country and liked to read books. She had gone to Columbia University, she wrote, to study Slavic languages. She had a particular interest in the Balkans, because of her family. Her father's family was Czech. Her great-grandmother, during the Nazi occupation, had been forced to prove, going back four generations, that there were no Jews in the family. Every family had to do this, and in itself it was not remarkable. However, during this process, Josephina's great-grandmother had unearthed some interesting family folklore, a story about two twins found under a pile of sticks in Bosnia in the early sixteenth century, and given the surname Hinterhölzer, *behind the sticks*. The twins, the story went, had been hidden to escape conscription by the Ottoman Turks. Josephina's grandmother, who had moved to America after the war, brought this history with her. Josephina wrote that she was told the story of the twins from an early age, but the strangeness of it did not occur to her until her late teens, when her grandmother had been dead for some time. Family lore is family lore, she wrote to me in the letter, and any actual case of two twins being found in a woodpile in sixteenth-century Bosnia was probably impossible to document. Nevertheless, she became interested in her supposed Bosnian roots, and the history of the Balkans. She returned home from Columbia and, with whatever free time and energy she had, pursued her studies in local libraries, contacted professors by phone and online, and so on. She did this—all the while alternating between periods of severe illness and relative reprieve—intensely for four years. Meanwhile, she traced her family back to a man in Prague who died in July 1789, just a few days, she added as a matter of coincidence, before the storming of the Bastille. Nearly three centuries of mystery remained between this man in Prague and the twins that the family had accepted as their progenitors. She saw her studies of the Balkans, she wrote, as an attempt to broadly construct a picture of the lives of ancestors whose identities were otherwise unrecoverable.

The Ottoman Turks, she wrote in her letter, conquered Bosnia by the mid-fifteenth century. Landowning Christian families were swift to convert to Islam, and in a very short space of time Bosnia had become an outpost of Ottoman civilization. Bosnian Muslims filled the ranks of the Ottoman military empire, and regularly raided surrounding Christian areas. The great Ottoman surge into central Europe, thwarted in 1529 and defeated in 1683, would go through this outpost. Every few years, the sultan in Constantinople sent warriors to kidnap the healthiest, handsomest Christian peasant children in the Balkans. In these so-called blood tributes, the raiders carried the conscripted children slung over the backs of horses, and took them in a convoy to the sultan. The mothers, grandmothers, and sisters of the stolen children would accompany the convoy for miles, weeping, exhausted, crying the names of the kidnapped, until they reached the river Drina. The Muslims carried the children across by ferry, and the families of the children could not follow. Some of the conscripted children performed military service, and the brightest of these emerged as top military commanders of the Ottoman armies. But most performed menial jobs, and life for them was over from the moment of conscription. Ironically, said Josephina in her letter, one of these conscripts would become the greatest Ottoman military leader in Europe, a grand vizier, and returned to Bosnia to build a bridge over the Drina. That bridge, wrote Josephina, is the subject of the greatest historical novel written in the twentieth century. During blood tributes, Christian peasants hid their children. And sometimes, if they could not properly hide them, they mutilated them, cutting off fingers or ears in order to make them unattractive to the sultan. If the story of the twins was based on truth — and, possibly, they had been hidden to escape conscription — the name Hinterhölzer would have identified them thereafter as Christians. Josephina wrote, I like to believe this is possible, but just as vividly as I can imagine someone stripping back those sticks to find two twin babies, given up rather than given away, I know it's possible that the story was invented, invented by a man, perhaps, trying to turn himself into Rome by giving himself Romulus and Remus—left to die as babies, found and suckled by a wolf, and raised as shepherds to create what would become the greatest civilizing force in all of history—as ancestors. She was disappointed that, as a result of her illness, she would be the last inheritor of this mystery, or at least the last person in whom the mystery was a condition in the blood.

I read the letter in a small white room in San Diego, three or four stories up, overlooking runways, with jets descending toward us in the dusky light, over the gold and green and calm Pacific, and sensed that I had become the first inheritor of the mystery not related by blood, and though I liked the idea of carrying something so enormous around in my thoughts, I had plenty of other things to think about. I was a few days away from becoming an ensign, and it wouldn't be long until my training began. I'd spend twelve weeks in OCS, then six months in nuclear power school, another six or seven months in prototype, then a few months in sub school. Then my first deployment. Josephina wrote that she had been following my progress in college through intermittent conversations that took place between my mother and her mother, but these could not have been very informative conversations, I knew, since I spoke with my mother just once a year, at Christmas. I have seen her only once in the past twenty years—and that was long after Josephina's death, when my sister gave birth to twins. I spent a few days in New York, where my sister lived, and took my mother to lunches. She would say things like, I wish we'd talk every day, like this. Or, I love you with all my heart. I would tell her there was no reason to say things like that, and that just because I didn't call or visit didn't mean I wasn't thinking of her, or didn't love her. You're like your father, she would say. My father was also in New York to see the twins. He had a good relationship with my mother still. They had simply realized she wanted a traditional life and he wanted something else. So they split, and he retired from his practice and moved to St. Croix. He bought a sailboat and found a black girlfriend, and he pretty much thought he was in heaven. He sent me a postcard that was a picture of his boat, full of rich people and champagne, and his black girlfriend, and on the back he wrote: Pig in Shit. It makes me smile to think that those were the only three words he ever wrote to me. And he did finally write them, and he was happy. He was dark brown when he arrived in New York, and he wore shorts and flip-flops everywhere, even though it was not warm enough for them. I picked him up at the airport, took him to his hotel — everyone else was staying with my sister — and then we went for a drink. He's Dutch — born in Amsterdam and moved to the US at the age of two; this is how I got a second passport. The concierge sent us to an Irish bar. We watched some weekday-night college football and caught up. I kept going out to smoke but he did not. He had quit smoking as soon as he arrived in paradise and realized he wanted to grow old. He was ex-Navy as well—a flight surgeon. We had not talked about my time in Iraq, before or after I was deployed, so after the game got out of hand—one of those games where Boise State is up on Idaho by five touchdowns in the first quarter, and nobody in America cares—I explained what I did. What was Iraq like? he asked. I don't really know, I said. I'd rarely gone outside the wire. I sat in a room and watched images of the war as though I were playing a video game by mind control, dozens of screens of the various areas of operation, some empty and some full of insurgents and, every so often, they would all be showing combat, and this was, a guy in my FDE said, like waking up in Satan's imagination. Sailors on sand, my father said. Cutbacks, war, et cetera, I said. Et cetera, he said. Do you think we can win it? I paused and looked at him. Never before had I been asked a real question by my father, a question that required my opinion, a question that did not already have the answer attached to it. For a moment I tried to think of something thoughtful, hard-fought, and profound, because I felt this was my one and only shot, and I imagined he might go back to St. Croix and say to his buddies, My son said *this*, and he was *there*; but I knew that if I did not tell the truth as I knew it, as I felt it, I'd fuck it up. I said, No, we can't win. They might, but we can't. He was drinking vodka on the rocks. He shook his drink. It was dry. He nodded at the bartender, then looked at me. I lifted my beer to the bartender. Thanks, I said. You bet, he said. A few seconds passed, and I said, You cannot map a coastline. He nodded. I said, They merely have to make us question our resolve, but we have to eradicate them. And I said nothing else about Iraq. He spoke briefly about the story of his own OCS training, which had lasted two hours and constituted no more than learning how to march, and I had heard it before, so I drifted toward the memories of my time there, and I asked those memories how the war would end. But they—these men sitting down in the hot sun, smoking cigarettes—had been fighting forever, and they did not understand the question. A lot of the guys I met in Iraq were insufferable nerds, idiots, bullies, or bureaucrats who could not function in the civilian world, where some degree of creativity is required. They all flourished in the military. But I also encountered the calm, stoic intelligence of the men who seemed less like human beings and more like discrete manifestations of the immortality of violence. They had fought at Thermopylae, at Gaugamela, and there they were, still, in Baghdad. It was, possibly, the fact that my role in the war was limited to watching it that fueled my romantic notions of these men.

We all stayed another few days in New York. I had grown claustrophobic—the flags, the cops, the taxis, the increasingly self-aware symbolism of American resilience — but it was nice to see my mother and father in the same room, talking about bullshit and admiring their grandkids. One morning, my mother, my sister, her two older kids, and I were in the kitchen. My sister's husband was at work — it was a Sunday, but he always worked. It was a cloudy morning, and the leaves had changed, and the city was loud. My mother was cleaning the counter-tops for the tenth time that morning, and my sister asked her to sit down. My mother said, Just a minute. Sit down, said my sister. My mother was wearing an apron. She searched for something to wipe her wet hands on, then wiped them on the apron. Hold on, she said. Sit down, said my sister. You want me to go? I asked. No, said my sister. I poured myself an orange juice and leaned against the counter. Mom, said my sister, I know you're busy at home, but I'm going back to work part-time soon, and I'd like you to move in and help with the kids. My mother pretended to address the problem of leaving, moving, responsibilities. Think about it, said my sister. The kids started screaming for her to move in. They pulled at her arms. I admired my sister. She asked no questions she did not know the answer to. She had a clear vision, not necessarily of what she wanted, but what she needed and how to get it. Her husband is a mean, greedy narcissist, with a thick New York accent and a sports car, and I'm sure he cheats on her, but when the marriage ends my sister will get everything, including the kids, and while he spirals into pathetic self-destruction she will find a way to be successful, proud of what she has accomplished, and remain a mother beloved by her children.

The day after that, my father flew back to St. Croix. My sister made me promise to get him to JFK so early that he couldn't possibly miss his flight. I drove him there and left him at the curbside, and he said, I've got three and a half goddamn hours, I'm checked in already, and I have no bags to check. So I told him I'd park and come in. That morning the clouds had vanished after a week of dull weather, and it was clear — the sky was light blue and bright, and there was a touch of winter in the air. You hungry? he asked. Not really, I said. So we sat at the bar of a Mexican restaurant and he ordered a vodka on the rocks. It's a bit early, I said. What does time mean to a guy who lives on a sailboat? he asked. Besides, how long's it gonna be before we get another drink together? Okay, I said, and I ordered a beer. We sat at the bar and periodically looked up at the television, which was playing what the bartender told us was a Puerto Rican soap opera. I had a feeling this would be the last time I saw him. Or perhaps I knew for sure. I think I may have tried to take a picture of him in my mind, to memorize him exactly, so that I would carry the image all the way to my death, and think of him then, as a man in his late fifties, happy, drinking with his son at an airport, so that I could tell his memory good-bye. I did that with everybody in my family. But if that is what I'd tried to do with him, and with the others, I failed, because I can no longer picture them—I see only disconnected parts of them. He's a tall man—six foot four, an inch taller than me—and he shaves his head. He wears cheap baseball hats and sunglasses indoors. My mother wears large, thick glasses and has a cackle, and my sister has blue eyes, which exist as blue and hazel speckles in the brown eyes of her children.

I was living in Norfolk at that time, temporarily, after my return from reservist duty—actually in a little motel on the interstate outside Hampton. I had come back from Iraq with a little bit of money and an idea. When my mother left for New York, I moved back to the desert and prepared to return to Iraq as a private contractor, putting my business together, contacting people, selling my strategy, organizing my visa, tendering for jobs, drawing up contracts, working out my security. Every dime I had, I invested in my business, and my apartment was the tiniest shithole you could possibly imagine. It was in one of those brown-wood, two-story blocks typical of that city, with a row of doors on the ground floor and a wobbly, uneven platform that you walk to reach the doors on the floor above it. I was on the ground floor. The light came through my green curtains in the way that daylight goes through water—underwater, you look up and see the light dappling and shimmering on the surface, but you look around and see the light is diffuse, and beyond it is a fathomless black mystery. That was what my place was like at times. I spent hardly any time there. I showered at a gym in the building where I rented my office. Across the street from my apartment was a halfway house, but except for the fact that they lived behind a high, barbed-wire fence, you could not have distinguished the inmates from anyone else in that neighborhood. Poor blacks and poor whites, poor Latinos. Addicts. Prostitutes. Thieves. Gangbangers. Dealers. Murderers. Drunk drivers. Rapists. They just sat on benches and smoked cigarettes, and from time to time a fight broke out. I had some upstairs neighbors, a couple of very tall teenage kids who lived with their grandmother on the second level of the apartments, and they and their friends used to stand along the platform, smoke weed, and stare at them. What are you staring at? one might yell. The kids said nothing. Who knew what satisfaction they took from it? Then another inmate would start cursing, just screaming at the bench he was sitting upon. Then a few more would start screaming at my neighbors, telling them to mind their own business. Then, when my neighbors refused to relent, a hysteria swept through the inmates. One woman might start repeating, No, no, no, no, *no*, *no*, *NO*, louder and louder, longer and longer, until it became the ridiculous and unnervingly comical sound of a child refusing to eat, and then another might start weeping, and so on. This could last hours. Only when the staff could get the last man to calm down did my neighbors withdraw. Nobody ever gave me much hassle. I stayed out of everyone's way. Perhaps they assumed, by the conservative cut of my hair, or the fact that I displayed no sign of madness or addiction, that I was a criminal of a higher class, the real fucking deal. Some Russian assassin. Or they may have simply considered me too dull to disturb. Things happened in that building that would horrify the average middle-class person. I mean beatings, assaults, daylight robberies. I ignored it. I didn't have a television or a radio, so I had to ignore it the old-fashioned way. I hummed to myself, or did push-ups. I had a girlfriend once who laughed at men who exercised to rid themselves of stress, and so I always laughed a little at myself doing those push-ups, but I was desperate. When there was nothing to do, I drank a lot of coffee. I had one of those Italian espresso makers you fill with water and put on a range, and I added cardamom to the grounds. The scent of cardamom reminded me of the coffee I drank in the Middle East, in Qatar, in Iraq, and my last hour there after my work on the FDE, in Queen Alia International, by myself, a sand-bound sailor on his way home, at the Four Seasons lounge, staring out the window toward the invisible city of Amman, which was buried in haze. I would travel right back through that lounge on my way to Baghdad as a civilian contractor. I must have gone through ten cups of coffee a day. Maybe that's what the average American drinks. Usually I was in the office from five a.m. to midnight. My apartment was just a few blocks from the football stadium, so near that on Sundays the roar of the crowd seemed like a great godlike breath trying to blow us over. I had not specifically sought a place by the stadium, but I liked living there, because it fed my hatred of the kingdom of ambitious stupidity, of the loud and gruesome happenstance of American domination. I hated that noise, and that stadium, and I hated everyone in it, and I sat for long periods of time on a couch I'd bought for nothing at a flea market, listening to the celestial ecstasy of the dumb luck of being born American. That collective whoop. I hated that country and every man and woman and child and bug alive in it. I had no idea what I wanted in life then, but I knew that I hated America, and I wished that it or I did not exist. And while I thought this, on Sundays, the stadium responded with great, ecstatic, dumb breaths. And when I went to my office, I dressed in a decent suit and put an American flag on the lapel.

About a month before I returned to Iraq, I got an email from Josephina's mother. It was one of those emails that say, I don't know if this address works, or if this is who I think it is, but I am so-and-so, and I know you from such-and-such, and I've been looking for you. I found you on the Internet. I was sitting in my office downtown, twenty-two stories up in a twenty-five-story building. It was around midnight. I had a nice view of the western half of the city, twinkling green and yellow and orange and red and blue and violet. The interstates made long white loops that carved the city into pieces. But for a moment, and I was never able to regain the sensation in a meaningful way, I realized the overwhelming blackness of the view. The sensation of suddenly noticing not only that the scene was more dark than light and more still than twinkling, but also that the darkness was far more intense than the lights, was like closing your eyes and opening them to discover that anything beyond what you perceive is attainable only in death. Beyond the outermost suburbs, where the black was most intense, the horizon rose into jagged, black, invisible mountains. There wasn't anything above it. Maybe one or two stars, maybe a planet. It had been a long, long time since I'd thought about Josephina, and when I remembered her letter I immediately remembered that I'd written back to her. I'd forgotten this for a long time. I cannot recall much of what I wrote to Josephina, and it may be that I was not supposed to write back, that I crushed the sentiment of her farewell in the same way you crush the farewell of a person who says good-bye to you on a street by continuing to walk with them. I believe I told her something like: I will pursue a destiny of justice and righteousness in your memory. I mailed my letter and became an ensign.

I telephoned Estelle immediately upon receiving her email, and the next day I drove south to meet her. It was my first trip home since I'd left. The drive takes about three hours. The landscape changes gradually from sand and dirt and rock and cacti and brush to sun-bleached grass fields, deciduous trees, milkweed, blue palmettos, and little flowers like rock lettuce and dandelions. You take the interstate south for a while, but you have to turn onto a small state highway that doesn't get much traffic. The day was warm and sunny, and incredibly bright. I really hated the place as a kid, and I had gone on hating it my whole life. In some ways I even recognized that what I really hated about America was the fact that I hated everything in proximity to this particular place, and the farther away I got, the less hatred I felt. It was like some kind of epicenter, but there was no event, no tragedy, no cause. I was born to hate the place I came from. That day, however, I fought a curious and unexpected nostalgia as I approached. I was thinking of what I'd say to Josephina when I got there, and I had to tell myself that it was not Josephina I would be seeing, it was Estelle. I listened to the radio. Mexican music. *Norteña* music. I stopped at a roadside stand and bought some dried chili peppers, not because I needed them, but because I wanted to get out of the car on the side of the road and stand in the sun.

I arrived around eleven. The town was as I'd left it. You hit a patch of houses built close to the road, many of them derelict—they were derelict when I lived there too. There's a gas station. Then you hit some tracks, over which the old downtown stands, where there is nothing but empty offices, empty rusted mills, empty rusted warehouses, and a tall, rusted water tank with the name of the town on it. The task of renovating the old town was too formidable, so they just left it to rust to death. Beyond it, there is an amorphous collection of houses down lonely, woody roads, then you come to a large highway, and past that a series of strip malls appears, and suburbs that drift back behind them. Josephina's house was not far from mine. I decided to speak with Estelle before I drove by my house. Estelle had not explained why, after all these years, she had suddenly looked me up, and until that mystery was solved I'd be too distracted to appreciate anything else. Nobody would be at my house. My mother hadn't got a decent offer on it before moving to New York, so she hadn't sold it. I didn't have a key. I just wanted to stand outside it for a little while, or walk around the front and back yards.

I pulled up at Estelle's and turned the engine off. At that time I was driving an old metallic-green hatchback Toyota—a car that was as beat-up and modest as my little apartment by the stadium. The house was a redbrick ranch-style bungalow with a two-car detached garage with an apartment on top of it, and a long but shallow screened-in porch. I do not remember the first day I ever met Josephina, but a photograph taken that day by my mother, in which Josephina and I are standing by bicycles outside that porch, hung on a wall full of pictures in our dining room. She had a green bike with a banana seat, and I had a black dirt bike. I watched the windows, on either side of the porch, for motion. It was a funny place to be, a funny thing to be doing. I pulled the keys out of the ignition, got out, and walked to the front door. I rang the bell and waited. There was noise, some footsteps, then the door was unlocked, then it opened. There was Estelle, short, a little overweight, with short white hair, wearing a red shirt and tan slacks. She shook my hand with both her hands, and she said it was wonderful and strange to see me again. I was so tall, so handsome. Come in, she said. We sat down in her kitchen, at a small round wooden table with flowers in the center and salt and pepper shakers in the shape of a rooster and a hen. It was only when I noticed these that I realized I was sitting in a shrine to farm animals. Ceramic figurines, from the thimble-sized to the whiskey-bottle-sized, crowded shelves on the walls, bookshelves, and filled display cases. Cows, pigs, sheep, goats, horses, chickens. The centerpiece was a large collection of photographs of Josephina as a child and teenager, which I did not linger upon.

Estelle served me some coffee. She saw that I was a little unnerved by the animals. It's what happens, she said. You collect, and one day you wake to realize you've turned your home into a mausoleum for your desire to have lived and died as a mother. She did not say that exactly. She may not have said anything at all. She offered me some food and I declined. I was starving, but I didn't want to eat in front of her. The coffee was weak. I took a sip and pushed it to the side. I'm glad you contacted me, I said. I'm surprised you came, she said. Me too, actually, I said. When was the last time? she asked. Christ, I said, who knows — was I sixteen or seventeen? She smiled and shrugged. We realized simultaneously that we had no personal connection to re-establish, and it seemed, therefore, pointless to go on avoiding the subject of Josephina. It's been a long time since I thought of Josephina, I said. I stood up and looked at those photographs. They were all the ordinary pictures of a child's life. I said, It's an incredible shame. She said, You and her were very close. Yes, ma'am, I said. I believe she was my only real friend here. She's the only person I ever missed. Estelle looked out the window at her backyard, which was large, green, and reasonably clean, and had not changed since the last time I was there. She said the same thing about you, said Estelle. Do you mind if I ask you something personal? I asked. Not at all, she said. Are you sick? I asked. She turned from the garden to me, in half astonishment, then realized what I was asking. No, no, I've been hunting you for years, she said. Ever since Josephina's death. Really? I asked. She said, You wrote a very nice letter to her. You read it? I asked. Yes, she said. I don't quite remember what I wrote, I said. I still have it, she said. I said, I'd rather not see it, to be perfectly honest. Did she say anything about it? Nothing, said Estelle, she just handed it to me and asked me to put it with everything else.

Estelle stood and placed both our coffee cups beside the sink. Did Josephina ever come to visit you, after you left? No, I said. Were you not boyfriend and girlfriend? We weren't, I said. Estelle put her hands in her pockets and walked very close to the back door, still looking outward. Whatever she wanted to ask now, she was not prepared to ask it. She seemed a bit embarrassed, so I said: I think I still have her letter to me. Would you like it? Estelle took her hands out of her pockets and crossed her arms. After a while she said, What was that? The letter, I said. I could make a copy. Yes, she said, that'd be nice. Then she opened the back door and said, Follow me. We walked outside, into the warm sunlight, and she said, Remember this yard? I do, I said, and it's strange to be back. I bet, she said. We walked to the detached garage. There was a little staircase that led up to the apartment's front door. There was a padlock on it. Estelle took a small key out, opened the padlock, then took out another key and opened the deadbolt. She turned the knob and opened the door. The door opened inwardly, and she stepped inside, and I followed. I cleaned a bit this morning, she said. All the curtains were closed, so the room was black, except for the oblique rectangle of sunlight on the floor that the opened door had allowed. She turned a lamp on. She'd had to replace the bulbs earlier that day, as well. The apartment was a single large room — a converted attic over the garage, with a sink and a fridge and a bed and a desk and an old television set. Boxes were stacked three high against the walls. She was fascinated by the past, by her family's past, said Estelle. Absolutely fascinated. If she had not been sick, I would have taken her to a therapist. I don't know why she set herself a task she knew she could not finish, and that nobody else would take up. What kind of struggle is that? She sat on the chair beside the desk and shook her head.

My memory of this day is tumultuous and murky. I do not trust a word of it. But a life is not a recollection of facts, and in Josephina's impossible task I saw something that was, if not heroic, then at least refreshing. Her mother found it absurd because she could not understand an obsession with facts. But nobody obsessed with the past is concerned with the facts. In her letter to me, Josephina had written: Truth has a qualitative, not a quantitative, value, and it is the very people ranting about the unattainability of truth who are most likely to utilize lies to squeeze, subjugate, undermine, and mutilate justice. So she lived here? I asked. Until she got too sick, said Estelle. Can I open one of these? I asked. Go ahead, she said. I went to a box and got my keys out and cut the tape open. A stiff scent of must and old paper came out of it. I dug through it. Amazing, I said. Maybe when I'm gone, somebody will want all this. Maybe some museum. Yes, ma'am, I said. So you weren't her boyfriend? asked Estelle. Well...I said. I only ask, she said, because she said you were her boyfriend. Estelle wasn't looking at me as she spoke, because this was no longer small talk. We were young, I said. I don't mind that, she said, not at all. Well, yes, then, we were boyfriend and girlfriend. Estelle smiled, still without looking at me, stood and clapped her hands softly. I realized I'd been pursued all these years to say the very thing I'd just said, which, of course, was not the truth, not in the way that she wanted it to be, but it was a lie I was happy to tell, if it brought Estelle some peace. She said, I wonder if you'd do something for me. Of course, I said. I wonder if you'd just spend a little while on your own here, while I sit in the house. I said, Ma'am? She was looking at her feet, which were tapping the dark-stained wooden floor. She could not speak, or would not. I closed the box. Sure, I said. I'll stay for a little while. She walked to me and took my arm and thanked me, and suggested that we say our good-byes there. Good-bye, I said. Good-bye, she said. She held my hand again with both her hands.

When she closed the door, I lay down on the bed and fell asleep. I'd been working sixteen- and seventeen-hour days for many months, and I was exhausted. I closed my eyes and slept through the afternoon. When I woke, it was nearly five p.m. I got up. I felt rested, but groggy. I had a cigarette. Maybe I wasn't supposed to be smoking. There were some glasses in the cabinet above the sink and I took one and used it as an ashtray. When Josephina had written me the letter, she was still living here, so what she said about noticing a place on the day you move in and out was, I supposed, a general comment about arriving and departing, connecting and separating. And I supposed that what she meant was that one's identity, while one lives in a place, is inextricable from that place, and only when the self perceives the place as separate does one see it as it truly is.

I drove to my own house after I left Josephina's. I parked a long way off and walked. I could not say whether I parked far away because I wanted to approach it slowly, or wanted to experience my old street as I had as a child, or both. The street was quiet. All the cars were gone or hidden in garages. There was, I realized, hardly a sound at all, and the whole world seemed to be slipping into darkness, superheavy, as though everything was being sucked into a point that existed in the center of my house— where nothing out of the ordinary ever took place, where there was no meanness, no neglect, no lasting sadness, no hatred. Yet the massive weight I seemed to attain as I approached it—a gray brick house with an elm tree in the front yard, and a long white driveway, shining in the blue and orange light of late evening, with shadows of a neighbor's trees stretched across the lawn — suggested an incomprehensible and impassable and monstrous guilt. It was a guilt that preceded me, that could not be denied or placated, and this was so real and agonizing that before I reached my house I turned around and got back in my car and left.

And it is this repulsive force I am pondering in a perfect calm, alone, smoking a cigarette, in Saskia's apartment. It is late afternoon, and already black outside. I'm in her bedroom, because her roommate is making dinner and Saskia has refused to let me go near him. She is in her en-suite bathroom, and steam is coming through the barely cracked door — the extractor fan does not work, she said, so she has to crack it. The room is dimly lit by two lamps with dark blue, almost opaque, lampshades. I am lying on her bed with my boots off — I left them in the cold and damp stairwell. My jeans are wet at the ankles, from the snow, so Saskia has put a towel down rather than make me sit on a chair. My shins, ankles, and feet are cold. It's the first time my feet and ankles have been cold in a long while. Otherwise I am warm. I'm still in my coat and scarf. My hat and gloves are beside me. The music on the stereo, Saskia told me, is a Spanish pianist named Mompou, who, she claims, was Chopin's only equal when it came to volume of sound in single notes. The music is slow, very slow, and seems to swirl and radiate in the dissipating edges of the steam coming from the bathroom. Saskia has been taking a shower for almost half an hour. She poured me a glass of wine and then poured herself a glass and went into the bathroom with it. And I lie here, imagining her wet arm reaching out from behind the shower curtain, feeling for the glass, bringing it in for a sip, then replacing it. This is the first time I've been in her apartment, and the building is as grubby as Janos, back in the café, implied. The stairwells stink. The paint is peeling and the floors smell of mildew. The walls are so thin you can hear the heavy front door to the building open and close, four floors down. Saskia's bedroom is messy and cramped, but in an eccentric, smart way. Books are stacked all over the floor, but her bookshelf is empty, suggesting that she is the kind of person who reads seventy-five books at once. In the stacks are the jagged, flopped edges of loose pages and stapled bundles of paper, which have come from years of evening classes. In many ways, she has admitted, she is not really reading books but working on thoughts, so that she might read a sentence in one book—a novel or a book of poems—and immediately need to leap to a history book, or an economics textbook, or an art book. Her small collection of paintings hangs on the four walls of the room. They are all so small that you have to get up and look at them closely to make sense of them.

Propped up on my little gray Samsonite case is the

painting we bought together. I still cannot tell which way is up, and I've forgotten the way Saskia has shown me. As soon as she is ready, Saskia and I are going to drop my things at my apartment and go find food. The woman — the landlord, or the landlord's agent, I wasn't sure — didn't want to give me the keys, even though I had my bank documents. I had expected this. Saskia and Manuela offered to act as my references, but she required references from landlords. So I gave her a year's worth of rent in cash. I went into the bathroom, pulled it out of my money belt, and placed the whole stack on the kitchen counter. I'd half hoped the woman might find it suspicious, but money is money. She smiled, took the keys out of her bag, and said, This one is the deadbolt to your door. This one is the door downstairs. This one is the door to the side terrace, and this one is to the bedroom's balcony. Saskia sat down at the kitchen table and smoked a cigarette. That was a lot of money to be carrying, she said. She was, I could see, disappointed after having seen it. I could not say if she was disappointed in me — because of the way I placed it on the counter, perhaps, like a gangster, or because of a suspicion on her part, which would have been justified, that I had added evil to the world in order to obtain it — or if she was simply disappointed by the fact that nobody could or wanted to resist money. I said, I just wanted to get this over with. This is why it's good to be rich, Manuela said.

We did not spend too long in the apartment after that.

Manuela, with errands to run, left us, and we promised we'd meet up at Chambinsky if we had the energy. I sat in my large living room, looking out the window to my small terrace, overlooking the cemetery, in a large, comfortable rocking chair, while Saskia paced around the apartment on the phone, trying to book a table for later. She came in finally and sat heavily on the couch. Every place she knew was booked out. She said, Why don't you go get your stuff and bring it here, I'll go home and change, and we'll meet in the city? I agreed that was the smartest thing to do, but as we sat there pondering the consequences of separating, we did not seem interested in that, either. There was always a chance we might get sidetracked, get tired, and decide to rain-check dinner, and for my part, continuing the rest of the evening without her had, without my realizing it, become unthinkable. So I suggested we stick together and see what happened, and when she agreed I could tell she liked the idea.

Mr. and Mrs. Pyz were sad to see me go, but our goodbye wasn't as emotional as I'd feared. They simply wished me well and told me to come back for dinner sometime. It was also easy to leave my little room. It might as well have been a bunk in sleeping quarters, for all the emotional attachment I had to it. Saskia came into the room with me, expecting to help me pack, and was shocked to see how little I had with me. When we left Hotel Rus, I turned around to give myself a chance to capture it in the condition of me leaving it, so that if I lasted in this city for another twenty years, I might think back on it one Christmassy night and remember the moment; but as soon as we left it the picture went hazy. We took a taxi to Saskia's place with my belongings. It was snowing again, though not as heavily as before. I was getting hungry, and was eager to head into the city, find a place to eat, then maybe hit another Christmas market, hear some music, and figure out a way to skip Chambinsky.

The glass door between Saskia's bedroom and the little shared balcony that runs in a square over the courtyard below is sweating badly with condensation. At the end of her bed, Saskia's clothes are piled in three huge mounds, which she classifies as dirty-and-to-be-washed, dirty-but-to-wear-again, and washed-and-ready-to-iron. She irons a piece of clothing only when she needs to wear it. She told me that she irons against the wall, since there is no room for an ironing board and no other uncluttered hard surface. Against the wall? I asked. Like this, she said, and showed me. There is nothing hung up in her closet, except hideous dresses she bought in a fever and is too embarrassed to return.

The shower stops. I hear the water dripping off her into the plastic-bottomed shower stall. I hear her open the shower curtain and step out, and I even hear the towel drying her. The Mompou is slow and quiet. There are times I assume it has stopped, then another note comes. Saskia opens the bathroom door fully, and steam and warmth billow out. She is wearing a towel around her body and another on her head. Is the music too dull? she asks. It's perfect, I say. She sits down beside me on the bed and throws the towel on her head onto the mound of dirty-but-to-use-again. She opens a drawer in a little chest beside her desk, and takes out some underwear and a bra. She lets the other towel fall from her body and exposes her back to me, an inch away from where my arm is lying. Her back is muscular. I can feel heat coming off it, after the shower. She puts on the bra and stands up, and ties the towel around her waist. She changes the music from the Mompou CD to some trashy europop. She taps her fingers along with the beat. You like this stuff? I ask. She walks to the bathroom again. You sound like Janos, she says. He can't stand the fact that I have base tastes. Maybe he knows his stuff, I say. She makes some noise in the bathroom, opening and closing a drawer, spraying deodorant, and returns with a blow-dryer and a hairbrush. Janos thinks his alternative music on his alternative station is art, and he thinks this is pop, she says. It's all pop. His music is just as predictable, just as sentimental, and nearly as catchy. The only difference, she says, is that this music does not pretend to be anything. And it's sung by people who are not pretending to be anything but petty celebrities. She plugs in the blow-dryer and sits back down beside me on the bed. Anyway, you can't hear Mompou over this, she says, and turns the blow-dryer on.

She's ready about twenty minutes later, wearing black tights and a denim miniskirt, a dark green, long-sleeve top, and an amber costume necklace. You look nice, I say. Do I? she says. We put on our boots in the stairwell, having completely avoided any contact with the roommate. Every stairwell in this city has the same overpowering underscent — a scent of wet stone. Nothing gets rid of it. Nothing even really masks it. Not plants or pots of potpourri or urine or mice or sunlight or shadow or breeze. Saskia's stairwell has it. The stairwell at Hotel Rus had it, and inside the lift too. And the stairwell in my new building has it. The woman who showed us the apartment stayed on her phone all the way up the stairs. I immediately wondered if the phone call, which seemed to express the fact that she was speaking to somebody else about the apartment, was an act, and wanted to tell her, as she clicked severely up the broad stone steps, that it did not matter, that if the place had walls and a ceiling, I was going to take it. She was a striking woman, less pretty in every respect but in every respect more beautiful than Manuela, not merely in aspect but in the air that came off her: She was stranger, more serious, more distant. I wondered if she spent time on her own after work watching people from windows, if she switched her phone off, sat down in a bar or café on her own, and wished she were another person, in another place. We arrived at the door to the apartment and she put the phone away. She turned around and waited for us all to arrive on the landing. She gave us an inauthentic, polite smile, one she did not even realize she was giving. She put the key in the door and asked us to step in. I went first, then Saskia, then Manuela, and finally the woman. The hallway inside the door was arched, white, and high, and had a small chandelier. The walls were wallpapered, and the wallpaper was old. Manuela and Saskia agreed that it would have to be redone, but I liked the way it looked. In fact, it was very much in line with the way I imagined it would have to be. There were two doors to the right and two to the left, and one straight ahead, which was the bathroom. The doors to the right were bedrooms. The first door to the left was the kitchen. The second was the living room. Every room had high ceilings, white walls, and a darkly stained wooden floor, except the kitchen, which was tiled. It was cold, but that was because the woman arrived only a few minutes before us to turn the heat on, she told us. Have a look around, said the woman. She checked the time on her phone and said, Take all the time you need. Saskia, perhaps sensing that I wasn't going to bother looking at all, took me into the kitchen. It was a large, rectangular room, with lots of counter space and a little island for chopping, above which pots and pans and large utensils hung from hooks. Beyond the island was a space with a large rectangular table. Beyond that was the flowerpot-sized balcony we had seen from the street. There was also a glass door in the far wall, with a view of the graveyard, that opened to a long, narrow terrace that stretched the full length of the apartment. It's nice, said Saskia. It sure is, I said. Let's check the bedrooms, she said. Manuela was in the bathroom, testing the water pressure. The shower came on — spurting once or twice, as the pipes in the wall shook and groaned, as though it had not been used in a long time. Manuela shouted, Good pressure! The guest bedroom was the same size as the kitchen, but, with only one window, which faced the street we had arrived on, was much darker. I only peered in. I had a feeling I would never be in there. But Saskia sat on the bed and said, as she bounced up and down lightly on the mattress, This is perfect. This is all I need. I left her there and went to the master bedroom, a large room with a big bed that faced some sliding doors that led to a small square enclosure. The curtains were drawn to either side of the glass doors. I opened them and stepped out. Saskia and Manuela followed. The little balcony, which had a high wall separating me from the next balcony, overlooked a pitifully dark and narrow space between the backs of buildings. There were wires and clotheslines and antennas, little plastic chairs beside flowerpots and small charcoal grills. Saskia looked over the edge. It looks like an Egon Schiele painting, she said. There were so many different shades of white and gray and brown and silver and black in that narrow space that it seemed like one very mottled and disconsolate color. Dots of contrast—hanging red shirts and yellow underwear and green sweaters—had grown icicles. I like it, I said. Some plants might cheer it up, said Saskia. It's north-facing, said Manuela. Nothing will grow but ferns. It'll be nice in summer, said Saskia, when you want shade.

I did not feel the need to check the bathroom closely, but when we crossed the hallway to the living room, I peeked inside, and saw a large tub, a gleaming white commode, and an oval mirror above a sink. That was all I needed to know—a bathroom of my own, with a tub big enough to lie down in. I would drag a little table beside the tub and put some books and a glass of cold water and an ashtray on it, and take the hottest baths I could bear. The living room was large and wide, and because of the width there was the illusion that this ceiling was higher than the others. It was maybe thirty feet long and twenty feet wide. That is not large relative to really large rooms, but compared to my little room in Hotel Rus it seemed like an opera house. Manuela sat on the couch and Saskia and I looked out the window. Beyond the long, narrow terrace and the two-lane street below us, headstones and mausoleums dotted a snowy, tree-filled hill, and beyond that the city rolled gradually downward, toward the river valley, and far beyond that were mountains, concealed by snow and fog. The woman drifted in behind us. That window, she said, gets the sun all evening. How long has the apartment been empty? Saskia asked. Not long, said the woman. The creaking and spitting pipes in the bathroom suggested she was lying, but that did not matter. Somewhere between the apartment and Hotel Rus, on the subway, on our way to get my things, Saskia asked, Does it bother you to be so close to a cemetery? How do you mean? I asked. People like to pretend they will live forever, she said. Oh, I said. She said, quoting, speaking from memory, slowly, Let us await it everywhere. I looked at her. She smiled. She was always in many places at once, invested deeply in a hundred different notions, and of all the things I liked about Saskia that was the thing I liked most. She took my arm in her hand, as though we were walking, and said, Such a long day. That repose, that sleepiness and quiet, accompanied her all the way to Hotel Rus, in Hotel Rus, and on the way to her apartment. She had her eyes closed often, and rested her head on my arm. The daylight was still semi-strong when we separated from Manuela, but had disappeared by the time we arrived at her place. Saskia was so tired I feared the end of her day had arrived, but the shower and a bit of wine revived her.

Now, in a taxi heading from her place to mine with my possessions, cruising slowly down the gritted and slushy streets back toward the city, in the darkness of evening, she is completely awake and excited again, pointing out things to see in her neighborhood. Places to get cheap rice, cheap fruit, cheap dry cleaning. Nobody wants to live in the area, she says, because of all the North Africans, but she loves it here. On many of the street corners we pass there are packs of young men standing in circles, reconnoitering with paranoid glances over their shoulders. They wear nothing but tracksuits — no hats, no gloves. They stand in heaps of shoveled snow, and snow falls upon them, and the wind gusts into their faces. We are going slowly, because the patch of road we are on is slippery, and under us the wheels of the taxi make a *zip-zip-zip* noise when they spin over ice. When the driver turns unexpectedly down a smaller street, Saskia knocks on the glass partition. The driver is North African. He looks in the rearview mirror. His eyes look at us, and they contain an aggression and dismay that is out of proportion to the two tiny beads held in that tiny reflective space that shivers as the car shivers, and he does not blink. She begins to speak with him, and he says something dismissive back, something that obviously shocks her, and she launches into him, nearly shouting, and I understand not a word, and then he raises his voice, and she leans back and throws her hands up, then crosses her arms, laughing out of disbelief. I told him he had taken the wrong turn, she says to me, and now he says I'm a woman and he isn't going to speak to me. Did he? I ask. I lean forward. Hey, man, I said. I knock on the glass. *Salaam alaikum,*

I say. He gives me a blank look. *Wa alaikum assalaam*, he says. I say, in English, How long have you been living here? Twenty-two years, he says, in English. I've been here six weeks, I say. I like it. Do you like it? I like it, he says. Are you from Morocco? I ask. I am, he says. How did you know? I figured it was Morocco or Tunisia, so I guessed, I say. What are you doing here? he asks. I tell him I've just moved to town, and just got a new apartment. He asks if I am working and I say I am not, that I used to work, but am retiring. Stress? he says, with a smile. Stress, I say. Could you do me a favor? He looks at me in the rearview mirror again, after having turned away for a while to watch the road. The look is fearful, like he expects me to finally say something confrontational. I say, Would you turn the music up? The music? he says. Please, I say. He turns it up a little — it's Arab music — and I say, Louder, please. He turns it up some more, and I say, Even louder. When he turns it up as loud as he can bear it, I say to Saskia, speaking loud enough to be heard over the noise, and slowly: I feel like taking the long way, and listening to loud Arab music. Saskia gets the joke, but after a while it doesn't feel like a joke. It just feels like a wonderful incongruity. I feel exceedingly tranquilized, and am reminded of another wonderful incongruity, on that day I arrived for the second time in Iraq, sitting in a convoy of white Suburbans cruising down the Baghdad Airport road to the International Zone. When I'd walked out of the plane and stepped on the tarmac in the heat, I realized I was not there with the Navy, and that I was in grave danger. I nearly panicked. Instead I chewed some gum and put on some sunglasses, and made myself look like a bored badass. At the airport, there were six of us — all civilian contractors — and we were separated and placed into three white Yukons with tinted windows. We had all received a long document about emergency procedures, and before we got into our vehicles a guy in black body armor, a crew cut, and red sunglasses went over the key points again. My heart was beating fast, and I kept my hands in my pockets so nobody could see them shaking. No one spoke until we were outside the airport, and for a few minutes after that, before we got properly on the road, it was just the security guys talking back and forth on the radio. Route Irish, the airport road, is twelve kilometers long, and initially traffic was sparse. It was a warm day in late spring, and the sun had turned the flat earth on either side into a shimmering silver sea of glare. In 2003 and 2004, guys in PMCs hung out windows and fired shots at cars that refused to pull over, or simply ran them off the road. Things had changed. We drove at an even, smooth pace, just slightly higher than the speed limit. We passed slow-moving vehicles and nobody seemed very anxious about it. The guy in the front passenger seat even took his eyes off the road to hook his iPod up to the radio, and played Jona Lewie's *You'll Always Find Me in the*

Kitchen at Parties. And then I felt that incongruity. I was calmed. I experienced a sensation of falling into nothingness. It seemed not at all like a spontaneous sensation but like a truth that had come a very long way, looking for me, knowing all I would think before I thought it, and shot me out of the sky. The rest of the journey passed without incident, but it took forever to get to the International Zone. The traffic congested. There was a noisy and impatient military presence. The road was heavily obstacled. Fences and barbed wire had been erected to keep cars and pedestrians from reaching the road by side streets.

As we drive, Saskia and I, in our taxi, toward the center of the city, I remember that a tour guide and amateur historian once informed me, when I asked where Baroque architecture came from, because almost every building in the center is Baroque, that it was essentially a happier, more theatrical and entertaining form of Renaissance architecture. Renaissance architecture, for its part, was a revolution from Gothic, or *Opus Francigenum*, as it was known then. It introduced a new vocabulary. Strange proportions and asymmetry were abandoned. The bewildering detail and staggering heights of Gothic cathedrals were replaced with clean semicircular arches and hemispherical domes. The leap from Renaissance architecture to Baroque, in comparison, was not a great one—just as the leap from Romanesque to Gothic had been small. Baroque vocabulary remained the same as Renaissance—classical shapes, symmetry, geometry, orderly arrangements—but the rhetoric had changed. It was a humanist, accessible rhetoric.

According to the historian, with whom I spoke after the tour he gave, in a little café across a small square from a little Romanesque church, which he said was the oldest operating church in the city, Baroque architecture was the first grand diminishment in human evolution in the West. He said that humanism was the victory of man's inner desire to be stupid in order to escape pain and to feel surprise, that the drive to re-establish classical literacy and eloquence had been impossible under the Catholic Church, and was doomed, in architectural expression, to be nothing more than naïve triumphalism, populism, and a retreat from intellectual honor—a retreat that would cost man everything, that would send human history spiraling into the abyss that would ultimately lead to modernity, from which there has been no escape. The historian was in his sixties, and wore circular, wire-framed glasses, and said all this very softly, without rancor, without even disappointment. Renaissance architecture, he said, born in Florence, could not travel. It was exceedingly difficult and inaccessible. It expressed human inconsequentiality. But Baroque, which was exceedingly easy to appreciate, and which expressed, as a deliberate lie, human significance, was like a plague, driven forth from Rome by wealth, or the pretense of wealthiness, and war, one hundred years of virtually continuous war in Europe, and colonialism, so that one may find as much Baroque in Mexico or Chile or even in the Philippines as one finds in France or Spain. Now mankind, said the historian, sinks forever into the despair caused by humanism and liberalism, which are nothing more than doctrines of flight from man's real nature. He fights wars to spread Enlightenment, democracy, freedom, rights, but what he spreads is a despair of which he is entirely unaware. I told the historian he should say such things during the tour, and he said he had, for a short period of time, become known for such tours, tours that took tourists into the heart of the crisis the city was, all around them, quietly expressing, locked inside the pretense of imperial majesty, reluctantly inhabiting the intimidating forms of absolute power. But after a few years people simply came to heckle him, and call him a coward and traitor. Once a man threw an egg at him. Once he was punched by a skinhead and called a Jew. So he decided to go back to regular tours, polite tours, and the more glorious side of history. Why didn't you quit altogether? I asked. Because I am a citizen, he said. I am a citizen. He paused, because my expression had not changed, and repeated: I am a citizen. He'd repeated himself with a tone of disdain that momentarily—though he would immediately go back to being polite—suggested my question was a hundred times more insulting than egg on his face.

After the historian and I had finished our coffee, he took out a huge map—a map that he stretched across the table so that it hung like an oversized tablecloth—and started drawing circles around streets where I would find exemplary works of late Baroque, and some authentic Renaissance. This took, embarrassingly, longer than the coffee itself—embarrassing because I had already shaken his hand, already wished him well. My mistake was to tell him that I'd moved here and had nothing in particular to do. We stood over the map, and the historian annotated the circles in handwriting I would never be able to read, and scratched his head, rubbed his eyes, and succumbed to a fever not unlike you imagine a great archaeologist might have succumbed to, suddenly aware he has stumbled upon the ancient tomb he alone believed existed. A waiter at one point asked us a question, and the historian did not so much respond as say, Ts! Ts! Ts! Ts! until the waiter left us alone. He circled a place where violins were once made and that is now a museum and a small venue for recitals. On Tuesday evenings, he said, the music school gave free recitals. So on the Tuesday that followed, I decided to go along.

I got there early and was told I'd have to wait. I was given a cheaply made black-and-white flyer with pictures of two young Japanese girls and a list of composers below them. I walked outside and smoked two cigarettes, and when I realized that had killed less than ten minutes, I walked around the block to look for a place to get out of the cold. I found an empty basement bar called New York New York. Inside, it was pretty dismal. A lot of purple light could not disguise the fact that in daylight it probably resembled an office cafeteria. A woman in her fifties, wearing a conspicuously conservative black skirt suit, sat at the bar by herself. I smiled and sat beside her, but left an empty stool between us. She spoke to me, and I stopped her immediately — I only spoke English, I told her, and I was very sorry about that. I ordered a glass of water and lit a cigarette. The bartender, an American, said, Hey, buddy, could you not spend a few bucks on a drink? He was maybe thirty, and wore a black bowling shirt with a pink collar. His hair was short at the sides and back and sort of spiked on top. He had the kind of American accent you have if you are born in New Jersey but leave when you're young, and live all over America. I said, Sure, I'll have a beer. Small or large? Small, I said. The woman fished a baby onion out of her cocktail. She threw her head back and held the onion above her open mouth as though it were a tiny little man and she were a giant lizard. She put it in her mouth, chewed, and swallowed, then turned to me and said, What do you tell an old hippy? I said, I don't know; what do you tell an old hippy? She delivered the punch line, which I didn't understand, either because she had slurred it or because she had momentarily departed from English, but I laughed anyway.

The bartender seemed to be happy I was there to deflect some of the woman's attention; he left the bar to wipe some perfectly clean tables, and he turned some music on. The first song was *These Boots Are Made for Walkin'*, and the woman got up off her seat and did a very slow and sexy dance against her chair. I watched her, because there wasn't anything else to do, nor anyone else for whom she could dance. When the song was over, she picked her chair up and moved it close to mine, and said, I used to be a jazz singer. Then she sang two words of a Louis Armstrong tune, gutturally: *I...see...* —I started coughing, loudly, the loudest cough I ever coughed, before she could sing anything else. The bartender returned. The woman held her empty martini glass up and said, Give me a whiskey or fuck me! Nobody said anything to that, and it disappeared into the pathetic darkness of the bar. She asked what I was doing here. Going to a recital around the corner, I said. I mean, what are you doing in the city? I began to say the usual thing I said, which was that I had no real reason, but that it seemed like a nice place, et cetera, when she interrupted me: What recital? I said, Just a free violin recital around the corner. Students. She looked me up and down. What are they playing? she asked. I said I didn't know. Someone had recommended it to me, and I knew nothing more than where it was. You're going to a concert, but you don't know what is playing? she asked. I remembered the flyer, and showed it to her. She pointed to the first girl and said, Kreisler, Glazunov. She looked under the second picture and said, Ah, *Ciaccona*. She said it as though she had suddenly become Italian. How much does it cost? It's free, I repeated. She said, Okay, I will go with you. The bartender, who had been polishing some perfectly polished glasses, stopped to see what would come of that. I didn't know how to respond, so I stuttered something out, just words like *maybe* and *um* and *well*. She turned angrily away and said, as though she were Poirot, casting accusations, Perhaps you only like teenage girls. I said, Well, it was nice talking to you. I'd finished only half my beer, but it was pretty tasteless. I walked out. It felt a whole lot colder, because I had not wasted enough time, and I had to go back to the recital hall thirty minutes early and hang around the front door like a creep.

The street was empty, but over a period of about fifteen or twenty minutes it began to fill with cars parking. Japanese people stepped out of them. The women carried large umbrellas—it was intermittently sleeting—and the men carried bouquets of flowers. There were young children everywhere. This was the crowd that developed around me while I waited. First there were five, then ten, and soon there were at least two hundred Japanese people standing outside the museum and recital hall. When they finally opened the doors, I was one of the first to go inside. The recital hall was a large white room with multiple thick white pillars and a vaulted sky-blue ceiling. There was a raised stage with a single chair on it, and a music stand. I took a seat in the front row. This seemed to annoy a lot of the people who subsequently filed in and wondered, I presume, who the hell I was and what I was doing there. I nearly stood up and went to the back row, except a man came out—a Professor Schmetterling— who obviously managed the recitals and taught at the school, and addressed us. For a while, nobody understood a word he was saying. He said, Would it be better if I spoke English? The Japanese crowd nodded and one man at the back shouted, Yes, please! So he introduced us to the evening in English. Tonight, he said, it is my privilege to present two of our most promising students. The girls were Umiko Chigama, age thirteen, and Shino Moroto, age fourteen. Chigama went first. She was very good, for thirteen. She was probably very good for thirty, but I would not really have known. There didn't seem to be any mistakes, though she played without much feeling. Moroto was better. She played the Ciaccona, or Chaconne, the fifth and concluding movement of Bach's Violin Partita no. 2. I believe I sat next to Moroto's father, since she looked at him while she was playing, and winked at him during applause. And since he wept when she played, and nobody else wept. Chigama had been very expressive—her shoulders dived from time to time, and her eyes rolled back. Moroto played with no expression at all, and seemed, at times, to mumble numbers to herself, but the music was somehow more powerful, louder.

When the recital was finished, I hung around in the hall for a little while. There was a large crowd around the exits, talking, not moving, and I didn't feel like walking through the congestion. And anyway, it was nice to sit and play some of the music back in my thoughts. When I had been sitting there for five minutes or more, Schmetterling approached and asked me what I thought of the evening. He was a tall, well-built man, with silver hair, obviously gay, and sat down when I said I had really liked the Chaconne. You've never heard it before? he asked. Never, I said. Do you know classical music? he asked. A bit, I said, like everybody. And then I realized where I was, and who I was talking to, and said, No, I wouldn't say I knew much. We chatted for a few minutes about what had brought me to the city, and the things I had seen since arriving. And I spoke a little bit about my past. He had a weird habit of saying the word *fascinating* in response to almost everything I said, as though I were explaining the solution to a problem that had stumped him for decades. Our conversation stopped for a few moments, and Schmetterling said: Speaking on the Chaconne, the composer Johannes Brahms, the most influential, greatest, and most profoundly visionary composer of the Romantic period, wrote to Clara Schumann—and here Schmetterling lifted his head, exactly the way Saskia does when contemplating — *On one stave, for a small instrument, the man writes a whole world of the deepest thoughts and most powerful feelings. If I imagined that I could have created, even conceived the piece, I am quite certain that the excess of excitement and earth-shattering experience would have driven me out of my mind.* Schmetterling then lowered his head and looked at me. I said that it was very good. He dismissed my comment with a wave. What you have seen this evening is a teenage girl with a little talent play it, he said. The Chaconne, said Schmetterling, which lasts about fifteen minutes, depending on the interpretation, was the supreme artistic achievement of the Baroque era, across all forms, and is without argument the greatest piece of music ever written for the solo violin. He looked around him. The room was almost empty. He seemed to want to express a sadness about the way people came and went. Someone waved at him and he lifted a hand in response and smiled politely. Returning to the Chaconne, he said, It's not just one of the greatest pieces of music ever written, but one of the greatest achievements across all human endeavor. When a real violinist plays it, the true breathtaking complexity of the piece becomes apparent. Bach was able to achieve a uniquely complex counterpoint — a conversation between multiple instruments — with a single instrument. He could do with many voices of a single instrument what another genius — I am speaking here of geniuses, only geniuses — could never hope to achieve with many instruments. Schmetterling leaned back in his chair, and checked behind him again. There were people standing and chatting at the back, and every few minutes someone would come to shake Schmetterling's hand and tell him he was a very good teacher. The Chaconne, he said, is technically one of the most difficult pieces of music for a violinist to play, but technically more than a few have mastered it. It is a requirement now for young musicians — in order to win a major competition, it must be in one's repertoire. In many ways it has become an important technical challenge for teenage violinists, and my students are always boasting about how this will be the year they learn to play it. It required, at the time of composition, every technique known to violin music, and not many techniques have been introduced since. What you have witnessed tonight, as I said, is a young violinist on the verge of competence. Competence, of course, with regard to the Chaconne, is nothing to be ashamed of. Yet a spiritual sympathy with the piece — which is not to say spiritual mastery, because no such thing is possible — is far more rare, and virtually nonexistent in violinists under, say, the age of thirty...perhaps forty. Today, there are perhaps three people in the world who can play it well. Schmetterling leaned forward, stood, walked to the music stand, and took the music that Moroto had left, perhaps in a nervous rush to get out of the spotlight, or perhaps it was not hers to keep. He sat back down and showed me the cover. This contains, he said, all of Bach's sonatas and partitas for violin. He opened it to the Chaconne, which was only seven pages long, and pointed to a line approximately halfway through the piece. Here, he said, in variation number forty, we see one of the most complex moments in the piece. Up to seven separate voices are in conversation here. He waited for me to respond, and when I did not he simply let a bit of silence pass, so that, perhaps, I could imagine the music playing in his thoughts. Then he said, It is really impossible to explain in words exactly how difficult it must have been to conceive this, not only as a line of music in itself but as part of a fifteen-minute musical conversation that is in many ways nothing more than a perfectly finite rearrangement of the constituent parts of this line. And these parts are nothing more — nothing more! — than variations of a single four-note theme that flow seamlessly into each other and are all four measures long. Do you follow? he asked. A little, I said. He nodded. One very interesting thing is the fact that Bach's theme — or we should say the essence of his theme — is an old four-measure bass line that was around long before he wrote his piece, and is still prevalent today, mostly in pop music. It was from this old and catchy foundation that he built his theme, and from that theme he built the Chaconne. You see, said Schmetterling, Bach was not an innovator. Nothing he wrote, at the most basic level, introduced a new form. In this way he is usually seen as inferior to Mozart, who in many ways was the supreme innovator, the supreme revolutionary. Mozart, at his worst, lacks feeling, but he is never sentimental. Bach, at his worst, is sentimental, grossly sentimental, but at his best he achieves an emotional expression that Mozart, the innovator, never dared allow himself to contemplate. Bach looked out across the landscape of music that had come before him and gathered it all up, every sound and every theme that ever existed, and to him they were bricks and wood and stone and glass, and he refined them into a musical cathedral that was unimaginable to anyone living in his age and unrepeatable to anyone after. The Chaconne, said Schmetterling, at least to me, combines in a single spirit the most extreme ends of a man's sacred and secular capacities. It is both a celebration of man and a proximity with God, or the story of how that might be possible, compressed into a single violin with many voices. It is a declaration of war on baseness and brutality and skepticism. But it was also written, quite certainly, in memory of his wife — he had been traveling, and returned home to find she had died. So it is a personal statement, I think, rather than a political one. Had it merely been political, said Schmetterling…no, it could not have been achieved. Without her death, I believe, the Partita might well have finished on the fourth movement, on the light and positive Giga. Instead, he plunges us into a profundity and intensity theretofore unknown in music. I also believe that the Chaconne — not alone but *by itself*, if you understand the distinction — resulted in the ascension of the violin as the most venerated of all Western instruments and, yes, the central cultural object in the West.

Schmetterling was going to end his lecture there, but he could see, I suppose, that I did not understand his last statement, so he continued. It is extremely powerful, he said. Fill a room with fifty different instruments, and have them all play a single melody. The only instrument you will hear, or at least the one you hear first, and loudest, if it is played correctly, is the violin. By the time Schmetterling said that, the room was completely empty. He gave me the sheet music and said I could keep it. Then he said, Tell me, really, what you are doing here. I said, I have told you. No, he said, tell me the truth. I felt some psychic wall crack under the weight of Schmetterling's strange, calm generosity, and I confessed: that I had assigned death from a distance, coordinated land and air attacks, missile strikes, and that I had, for a reason that is still beyond explanation but was, until then, the most necessary thing I ever did in my life, returned to Iraq alone. Had I intended to make restitution? Had I gone merely for money? Had I gone to get myself killed? Or was Iraq the only place in the world where I could find some equilibrium—where the world hated me as much as I hated it and myself, where I could live in the safety of never-ending hatred? It did not matter, I told Schmetterling, because I had only done harm. I left, finally, after a long stint of work with the Iraqi police. I was helping solve a string of kidnappings and murders of policemen and translators working with the US Army. For this, I had essentially reprised my role as a naval officer in Baghdad, except I was a one-man team. I did most of the work in my hotel room. I woke, made some coffee, went online, checked email, checked the intel I was getting—the Army was providing a lot of it—checked surveillance activity, and prepared reports for the Army and police. These were long days. They were so long I had to phase out all the other work I was doing, all the reconstruction and development consulting. There was no more rescuing priceless artifacts looted from museums. From time to time, I left the Green Zone to meet with police officials in places where abductions were heavy, and on occasion I went out to Forward Operating Posts to give briefings about progress on our cases. The insurgents were abducting these men and torturing them to death. We knew this because we found the bodies. The interrogations, based on the conditions of the bodies found, often took a very long time. They squeezed the men's heads in vise grips until their skulls broke. They broke men's backs. They sliced off limbs and genitals. They poured acid all over faces.

They—and this was true—tied them down, made small lacerations all over their naked bodies, and had housecats chew on them. So the men I worked with—the forces I helped coordinate—were eager to reduce the abductions for the sake of getting new recruits. The US Army was keen to identify and halt the leaks that were leading to the security lapses that allowed these men to be abducted—the identities of translators, for instance, were supposed to be kept secret. The Iraqi police said the same thing—that they wanted to reduce abductions, identify leaks, and boost the morale of recruits—and perhaps they meant it, but in reality the only deterrence measure they could carry out with any efficiency was to retaliate with torture nearly as extreme as the insurgents'. One morning, at a police station in southeastern Baghdad, I was briefing a chief inspector and a US Army lieutenant colonel when there was suddenly a bit of panic. A man came in and spoke to the chief inspector, and the chief inspector immediately excused himself, put all of his papers into a case, and hurried out the door. The lieutenant colonel, now freed of his obligation to be respectful to everyone in front of the Iraqi chief inspector, responded with a *fuck off* when I asked what he thought that was all about. And then I was all alone in the blank little room, except for a little table with some orange soda cans on it, and a platter of chocolate bars. I got my things and left, and went out to the main room where all the desks were, and where small oscillating fans blew air around slowly, and sat down across from the only man still there — there were, because of rampant attacks on police stations, often very few men inside them — an inspector who was leaning back in his chair and smoking. Rather than rearrange my lift back to the Green Zone at great expense to myself, I just sat down near him, lit a cigarette, and asked how things were going. Fine, he said. What was all that about? I said. He leaned forward, and I leaned forward too. He said they'd got a high-value target and were taking him for questioning. I asked why the questioning didn't take place here. I knew the answer. Perhaps I asked the question because I wanted to pretend to him or to myself that I did not know the answer. The inspector smiled and leaned back again. He said, cryptically, and in an English so broken and so mispronounced that I had to rephrase his words in my mind as he spoke, or rather speak for him: The way to win a war is to convince your enemy you have the right to kill him. The enemy will fight forever, to the very last man, if he believes his enemy has no right to kill him. When our men, he said, are abducted and tortured, what are they asked? Nothing. It's punishment for working with collaborators. If they want secret information about the Iraqi police, he said, they can walk up to the first policeman they see, give him a little bit of money, and ask him a question. If they want an Iraqi policeman to assassinate somebody, or let them drive a bomb into a crowded square, easy, they just have to pay him. That was the inspector's answer to the question of why the man was not being questioned in the station. Of course I knew that nobody of any importance was ever questioned in a police station. I checked the time. I had a while still. I leaned forward again and, out of real curiosity, not in an attempt to make a moral accusation, asked, What's it like, getting someone to recognize that right? The man leaned forward and said something like, I suspect you know far better than I. Perhaps he said another sentence entirely. Perhaps he said it was rewarding. The man leaned back and said nothing more, and I decided it was worth the expense to get my lift back to the Green Zone rearranged.

I looked up at Schmetterling. I wasn't sure how long I'd been talking, but the room was darker and I felt guilty about keeping him there. I also felt that, having heard what I had to say, he had good reason to want to get away from me. Schmetterling wasn't looking at me. He was looking at his own crossed knees. And when I finished speaking he patted my shoulder, still looking down, and I was thinking of the Iraqi curator who had wept over an artifact, and my own desire to do something to reassure him that I believed in his right to weep over a thing, though there, in front of Schmetterling, I felt no need to weep over the man they'd taken that day. We stood, Schmetterling and I, and walked out, and he said good-bye to the girl who was sitting in a booth beside the entrance, and who would presumably be locking up. Schmetterling and I walked together toward the subway. It was still sleeting, but Schmetterling, not surprisingly, had a gigantic umbrella. We made small talk for a little while. The sidewalks were slippery, and Schmetterling wore leather-soled shoes that required an absolutely snail-like pace. But, he said, picking up the previous conversation without any warning, you may be surprised to hear that the violin was not, originally, a Western idea. Yes? I said. Indeed, said Schmetterling. Well, perhaps the violin itself—what we today know as the violin—was first produced in Italy, in Cremona, in 1555, probably by Andrea Amati, though it is also possible that Gasparo da Salò invented it. The most beautiful and arguably most famous violin ever constructed, by da Salò in 1574, was made for Archduke Ferdinand II. This Archduke Ferdinand, said Schmetterling, was an interesting character, because he collected and adored art, but he also led one of the most brutal campaigns against the Turks, a campaign that took place not too far from here, in 1556. Which is ironic only insofar as the instrument he would cherish among his most prized possessions had come from that direction. Schmetterling saw that I finally understood what he was talking about, and paused for a moment to let the recognition soak in. You see, he said, the idea of a small, stringed instrument that could be played with a bow came to Europe first via the pear-shaped Byzantine lyra, and secondly via the boat-shaped rebec, which the Moors brought to the Iberian peninsula in the eleventh century, and which, in some models, could be played while held under the chin. The rebec's predecessor was the rabab, a medieval Arab two- and three-stringed instrument from the ninth century, which is likely the predecessor to the Byzantine lyra as well, and therefore the single precursor to the violin. And all this interests me, said Schmetterling, especially this evening, because the Chaconne, which I believe to be the greatest piece of music ever composed, argues for a Western ideal, and justifies, in its own way, Western dominance of science and art and light and combustion and music and trade, and the embryo of the instrument used to argue this—the only instrument, ironically, capable of making this argument—emerged a very long time ago in a most decidedly un-Western place, had a one-octave range, and never dreamed of what it might become. We arrived at the subway station and discovered that we were going to be traveling in opposite directions, so we shook hands and he suggested I return to the museum in daylight, and try to find a good recording of the Chaconne to listen to, and perhaps even buy a book on it or Bach or music of the Baroque period. There was, conveniently, a shop in the museum where I could pick one up.

The taxi arrives at my apartment, and I grab my things and pay the driver. I have already forgotten which key is for which door, and my hands are shaking from the cold. Saskia is bouncing up and down with her arms crossed, saying, I think it's that one, I think it's the other one, it must be the last one. The door opens and we head inside. The corridor is cool. We head up the steps and arrive at my door. So, she says, this is your new apartment. I say, Pretty cool. I open the door and we walk in. I drop my bags by the door and immediately realize that if we stay longer than five minutes, we're not leaving. I say, Let's get out of here as quickly as possible and get something to eat. She must be thinking the same thing, because she says, Sounds good. I change shirts and wash my face and brush my teeth, while Saskia, without taking off her coat or shoes, paces the big hallway. We leave the apartment. The night sky is green and pink, and it pours forth heavy soft snowflakes. There's a bus stop on the road with the cemetery, so we walk to it and wait. The bus arrives after about five minutes, and it's empty, but the floor of it is covered in water that feet have carried in as ice and snow. Those feet have also tracked in sand and grit. The inside of the bus is exceptionally cold, because the heaters are not on, or are broken, so we sit close together in our coats and gloves and scarves and hats, and we can even see our breath, and Saskia's teeth are chattering.

The journey from my apartment to the center is nothing, not even ten minutes, and just a few streets past the ring road Saskia presses the button to stop and says she has remembered something I have to see. She adds, Another thing you have to see. The bus stops and we alight. The air outside seems strangely warmer than the air inside the bus. It is a quiet street, but shimmering in red and green and crystal-white light from enormous Christmas bells that hang everywhere. From another street, music plays. The bus drives away, through the slop of snow and grit and ice. And we walk another direction, through the same terrain. Saskia says, You must pass through this place. What place? I ask. Come on, she says. The road the bus has taken without us goes jaggedly up-ward, and we walk along the base of a steep and tall rock face that had once been a natural part of the city's old wall. A narrow switchback stairway has been carved im-perfectly out of the stone. Saskia says that on a cold night a long time ago a young and unknown poet, ascending this stairway, saw a woman with large eyes and white cheeks descending. Until that moment, he despised ev-erything he knew, all the people he had met in his short life, and longed for the sack of the city and its consump-tion by fire. But at that moment, said Saskia, he decided that what he had felt all along was an extreme form of unworthiness, rooted in sexual desire and lack of fulfill-ment. The woman passed him, but not before she glanced at him with eyes so blue they were silver, then she dis-appeared down the steps, and walked, quietly, along the frozen canal circling the city wall. He immediately went home, composing, in his head, as he hurried through the city, a poem about the experience, and when he got home he told his roommate what had happened. The roommate went to every door in the building and demanded silence. When the roommate returned, the poet was in his room, working. The next morning, the roommate awoke to a knock on the door. It was all the tenants in the building, who demanded to hear the poem that would reignite love in their hearts. The roommate then discovered the poet had slit his own throat in the night. He was lying in bed, covered in blood, and the blood had saturated his sheets and formed a large puddle on the floor. He left a note in which he explained that he had discovered, in the hallucination of three or four a.m., that his unworthiness was perfect, and any accomplishment or happiness would corrupt the perfection, that he must die a virgin that very night, before the sun rose. As for the poem, according to the note, he composed it and ate it. It was twenty-four lines long. He was seventeen.

Is that true? I ask. Saskia's response is: What matters is that this stairway became, for our poets, the center of poetic purity on earth. And no poet from here, major or minor, becomes a citizen until he or she has composed a poem about this stairway. Even the anarchists and Symbolists wrote poems about it, all twenty-four lines long. To be a citizen is the highest ambition of the poet. Citizen, she says, and I cannot remember if I told her what the historian said and this entire account is a response to that, or if it is just a coincidence. We reach a landing where the stone wall is covered in graffiti, tiny and intricate scribbles. Here, says Saskia, is hallowed ground for poets. It's where the amateurs come to praise the young poet. The purpose, she says, is to subordinate oneself, to declare your inconsequence to the whole world.

We continue upward. Snow covers every step thickly, and our feet make those great soft noises that feet do in deep fresh snow. No one has come this way for hours, at least, though I can hear a lot of noise from above. It is the sound of oblivious gaiety, shouting and singing and mechanized bell noises. A Christmas market? I ask. The best, says Saskia. We arrive at the top. The market is situated between two vast museums that face each other. There are bright amusement rides, a merry-go-round and a flashing Ferris wheel. Let's go through it, says Saskia. There is a children's choir singing on a large stage and, in a beer tent, about fifty men in Santa Claus suits, looking inappropriately sober. Everywhere else, the square is festive. People are drinking hot wine and stuffing their faces with sausages and pastries covered in confectioners' sugar. Saskia suggests we scrap our plan to have a nice dinner and eat something in the market. That sounds to me like the best possible idea. The prospect of sitting down somewhere dark and quiet and being forced into an intimate conversation is completely unattractive, especially since I know that kind of conversation would lead to the question of what I plan to do on Monday, Tuesday, Wednesday, Thursday, Friday, and so on. The children's choir is really awful. But they are having fun, and lots of people have circled around to watch them sing. And when they get any melody halfway right, the crowd cheers. I buy a small box of overpriced, gourmet green tea, throw the box away, and stuff the bags into the inside pocket of my coat. Green tea seems like a good first grocery item for the apartment. Something I can drink nonstop, unlike coffee. There are a lot of things here that I suddenly feel I'd like to buy, but I don't want to have to carry a bag around for the rest of the night. For our dinner, we find a hut that serves hot sausages sliced on paper plates, with sharp mustard and brown bread, and we eat while standing in the cold. Saskia gets a drink after that, and I get a second plate of food, and she holds her mug in one hand and covers it with the other, to protect it from the snow. The crowd flows past us, and no matter where we move, we keep getting jostled. Some people are polite about it. Others are rude. In an attempt to find a comfortable and calm spot to stand in, we drift until we find ourselves standing beside a metal barrier between the market area and a cluttered parking lot of caravans and cigarette-smoking cooks and vendors. Beneath our feet are crushed and crumpled plates that have fallen out of a nearby, overfilled trash can. People, seeing there is no more room in the can, throw their trash at our feet. I pull the metal barrier back and walk through. Where are you going? she asks. I don't know, I say, but I don't want mustard on my new coat. She comes through with me and I close the barrier behind us. There is a nice emptiness and calm back there, but without the crowds it seems a degree or two colder.

Some of the men in Santa Claus suits start digging through the bowels of two black buses, pulling out instrument cases. You know, I say, maybe I ought to try and learn an instrument. Which instrument? she asks. What about the violin? I ask. Saskia shakes her head. Too predictable. Everybody here plays the violin. I like the piano as well, I say, but it's too big. I want something I can carry. What about a guitar? she asks. A classical guitar? I ask. Exactly, she says, with twelve strings! And for a little while we go through a list of every small instrument we can think of. The Santa Clauses take out their instruments and prepare to step on stage. When I was very young, maybe ten or eleven, my mother took me to guitar lessons. She bought me an electric guitar, and though I liked sitting down with it, and looking cool, I disliked playing it. I never practiced, and when I went to lessons, the teacher, whom I remember now strangely with some specificity, who had a salt-and-pepper beard, long hair in a ponytail, and wore, at least in my memory, nothing but red T-shirts with little breast pockets, sighed and sighed and sighed at my lack of interest. These lessons took place in a tiny white room he must have rented in a little strip of offices on the side of a road. I remember it was undecorated, as though he were one of many tenants. My mother drove a station wagon—a yellow Chevrolet with wooden panels—and my father drove a burgundy Jaguar XJS. Often, though, they swapped, because my father loved the station wagon. I remember various days of packing that guitar into those cars and fretting that I had not prepared even ten minutes for the new lesson, but lying to my mother that I had. These memories are sure and clear, yet I could not say how many months the lessons persisted. It must have been a while. One day, in a moment of frustration, the teacher took the guitar out of my hands and packed it in the case, and the two of us sat there in silence for a very long time. I was ten or eleven, and he must have been in his forties. We sat on the only two chairs in the room, facing but not looking at each other. And when our time was up, he said to my mother that he had to discontinue teaching me and wished me luck—that last session was free. When I think of my childhood, I remember it mostly as a series of attempts by my mother to get me interested in things. In one of her more desperate acts, she spent a lot of money on a set of encyclopedias and demanded that I file a verbal report to her every day on a new subject. After a week of feeling very silly reporting obscure facts about distant

countries or scientific discoveries to my own mother, I refused. So my father bought me a motorcycle. I wrecked
it and broke my leg: I hit the only tree in a big, grassy
field. It was a little 80cc Yamaha that did about forty-five
miles an hour, with an orange tank with a white racing
stripe. I drove straight at the tree for a long time, and
had intended, I think, to veer away with inches to go, to
make a death-defying escape. I don't really know what
happened. I lay on the ground for a long while afterward.
I was in a lot of pain, but I was not afraid. I felt bad for
my mother, who would blame herself, and my father, who
would blame himself, and if my leg had not been so badly
damaged that I could not walk, I would have gladly gone
home without telling anyone — curiously the bike seemed
unharmed. But the accelerator was stuck in the dirt and
the engine was screaming and the back wheel was spinning and gray smoke was spitting out of the little exhaust
pipe. It was so loud that it attracted attention. I propped
myself up on my elbows and saw a man — just a guy who
happened to be around at the time — sprinting across the
field toward me. What a sight he was. For years I saw him
in my dreams, that figure, frantically running. My memory loses sight of him beyond that. I have no recollection
of him reaching me, or speaking with me, only of him
running, only of him coming for me.

The snow gets heavier, and Saskia and I decide to de-
part. We walk in no particular direction, but always tend-

ing away from the apartment. And in our wanderings, during which we speak very little, except to say how thick the snow is in places, or comment on the vision of the cold, still city at night, which seems to me intensely beautiful around every corner, my heart shrinks and expands a hundred times, expanding and shrinking at the realization that tomorrow I will wake as a citizen of resignation.

Later, much later, a little after three a.m., at home in bed in my new apartment, I find myself unable to sleep. The night is over. Saskia and I arrived at Chambinsky around eleven o'clock, after she started receiving messages on her phone from Manuela. The memories of the walk from the Christmas market to Chambinsky, from where I am remembering it now, come back to me like pieces of a smashed mirror, some dull and some glimmering. We stopped in a bar to get warm. We watched some kids sledding down stairways on large metal street signs. We walked across an old bridge with statues of saints on it and a bench upon which Saskia had slept one night, drunkenly. In the days when she could sleep, she told me as we paused at that bench, she could sleep anywhere, and for as long as she liked. The bench on the bridge was just an example. For years—this was when she first returned to the city—she liked to fall asleep on park benches. She said, Nobody knows this about me. What happened? I asked. She said, I was mugged, and I figured I had got lucky. We turned a corner at that moment and found ourselves on a small street—there seemed to be nothing but dark windows and gray stone, and suddenly, from a single spot in the long monotonous darkness, there was a bright light and some noise, with a magnificent intensity, as though the light and noise were splitting the stone open from the inside. We walked in the middle of the street, because it had been plowed, and Saskia's heels made huge echoing cracks on the road. Then we were at the light. This is Chambinsky, she said. Saskia opened the door and sound tumbled out at us. I was thinking, at that moment, that nine or ten hours before, when the idea had first been proposed, I could think of nothing worse than hanging out with a bunch of people fifteen years younger than me, introducing myself over and over, being a foreign nuisance or a foreign curiosity. But slowly that worry had diminished. By the time we arrived, I was looking forward, finally, to a drink, and Saskia, who was in a good mood, which had put me in a good mood, wanted to see Manuela.

The front room was very brown. There were wooden chairs and wooden tables. All the tables were taken, and all the seats, and people who had arrived too late to get a seat were standing in the large space between the tables and the bar, which was long and narrow. Do you see them? I asked. Saskia squinted, scanned the tables in the front space, and said she didn't. She took her phone out and telephoned Manuela. They spoke for a few seconds, and Saskia turned and looked toward the back of the building. I followed her line of sight and saw Manuela, on the phone, waving. The space at the back, where the old theater must have been, had tall, tall ceilings, too tall, in fact, to see them from the front bar, and there was a haze of the sort you sometimes notice in big hangars, which has a hum to it — not the space itself, but in your ears when you look at it. We took our drinks and walked to where Manuela was. When you came out from the front space to the back, you got a real vertiginous shock. To the left, there were pool tables, all in a row, more than a dozen of them. To the right, in a far larger space, were lots and lots of picnic tables covered in oilcloth. We had to walk right through the middle of the crowd. The boys wore beards and mustaches, T-shirts and ragged sweaters, little hats and cool glasses, and I felt like they were looking at me with the same mix of shame and animosity they might show if their fathers had suddenly walked in. The girls didn't seem to be looking at me. Manuela was with a large group crammed around a single large table. I guessed she thought Saskia and I were in love, because she bore an expression of that friendly pride you feel when someone you like has found happiness. I didn't get the sense that Saskia went around thinking about love much, or pursuing it. I gathered, having heard the story about her father, that she would always suspect that love was a kind of repulsive, debilitating madness, that, far from being the source of ultimate happiness, it was extreme unhappiness masquerading as happiness, a temporary euphoria that felt wonderful for a little while, then killed you, like freezing to death. Of course that's not the truth. I imagine that Mr. and Mrs. Pyz are in love. I imagine that love is everywhere. I imagined, in the big room through which we walked, that love was teeming, that it spilled out of the pupils and mouths and teeth and tongues of more than half the people there. I imagine that love is some people's whole reason for wanting to live. We arrived at the table. Manuela said, I'm glad you came! Saskia said, We've walked the whole city, it seems. The others did not pay us too much attention. They glanced, but they said nothing. Janos gave me a nod. You went shopping, he said. New coat, I said. It's nice, he said, but you look a little like Adolf Eichmann. I looked at myself. Janos hadn't intended the remark as an insult. He really meant it. He was probably right. In a few years, I said, it'll be dirty and threadbare. Janos shrugged. His friend said something to him, and he turned to speak with him, and forgot us. No one else made room so we could sit. There was not room to make, really. Every inch of the table's perimeter was covered with arms and elbows, and scooting out was impossible, since every table was like that, and the space between tables was small. Maybe, at a stretch, they could have made room for two good friends, but I was a stranger, and whoever got stuck beside me would have to speak with me, in English, and come down from the bliss of effortless and pointless chitchat.

Let's play pool, said Saskia. But all the tables are full, I said. She said, We just put some money down and wait. Do you play pool? I asked. No, she said, but it's better than standing. Manuela said, I'll come along. And all the guys noticed this, because Manuela, simply by being so beautiful, legitimized them as a group. The three of us went over to a table where a bleary-eyed guy with a mullet and a wrestler's mustache was standing unsteadily over a freshly racked set of balls, holding a bottle of beer. Saskia spoke to him, and he answered. What did he say? He said you look like a Nazi. I looked at Saskia and Manuela. Why didn't you tell me I looked like a Nazi in this coat? You don't, said Saskia, you look nice. Manuela said, If you're not wearing a T-shirt, people in Chambinsky accuse you of looking like a Nazi, but if you left your coat on a chair, they'd probably steal it. Will he let us play? I asked. The guy said, in English, Play you for a tenner. For money? I said. Yes, he said, I will break. So we played him. It started out as me and Saskia versus him, but he was so bad, and so drunk, that I let Manuela and Saskia play him, and I just stood and drank my beer. At one point I think fifteen minutes passed without a single ball being potted. Why did you want to play for money? I asked the guy. Because I hate Nazis, he said. A little while after that, Janos came

over with a friend and said, This is Zaid. He doesn't believe you fought in Iraq. Hey, I said. I put out my hand
for Zaid to shake it, and to my relief he shook it. Nice to
meet you, I said. So is it true? he asked. It's true, I said.
Then I said to Janos that I thought I wasn't supposed to
say anything about it, and Janos said, But now we've been
drinking. At that point, Manuela shrieked. She'd potted
a ball. Zaid said, I'm a journalist. Newspaper? I asked. I
write for a website, he said. I'm the editor. Well, I said, I
don't imagine I could tell you anything about Iraq you'd
find interesting. I don't either, he said, I just never met
anyone who fought in a war. I'm not in the military anymore, I said. Nevertheless, he said, in a way that made me
think that when he spoke English he overused the word.
I said, So, what do you think? I thought you'd have a bigger jaw, he said. Another one of Janos's friends came over,
and I suddenly felt it was a good idea to go have a cigarette outside. Saskia and Manuela still had a few balls on
the table, and it did not appear that the guy with the mullet had hit one in yet, so I told them to make sure they
got the money if they won while I was away. Saskia came
close and said, Are they annoying you? Not a bit, I said.
You're not leaving? she said. Of course not, I said.

I went out to the smoking area with my beer, and stood
in a huge, drunken mass of handsome young people. To
find a comfortable place to stand and smoke, I had to
go all the way to the barrier and lean my arm over it. It

seemed to me they could have moved the barriers two or three feet farther out, though that would probably just bring more people out. All over the place, propane heaters burned orange and hot, and people took turns standing under them. Beyond a few meters the heat evaporated, and where I was standing, trying to light a cigarette with my gloves on, it was frigid. Saskia had said it was going to hit minus fifteen that night, which was a whole lot colder than it had been. I got the cigarette lit, and was just standing without thoughts, a little tired, when from out of the bar and into the smoking area came two American guys and one girl. I heard them a long time before I saw them. I thought of Schmetterling and the violin, and the way American accents rise above all others—that if you put a hundred nationalities in a room and asked them all to complain about the lack of customer service, the overweight woman from Ohio will be the one that shatters the nearest chandelier. The three Americans who walked into the smoking area were bad enough that I could hear every word they were saying. I figured they might be exchange students. The girl had short, ice-blonde hair. One guy wore glasses and had a beard, and the other wore a baseball cap. They looked about twenty, each of them. At twenty, I might have been even more conspicuous, I reminded myself. I tried to ignore them. I had about half my cigarette left, and I wanted to enjoy it by returning to my lack of thoughts—

but just as I had been forced to the spot where I stood, they were being forced to the spot where I stood, and there was not a whole lot of room. The guy with the baseball cap wore a black leather motorcycle jacket. The girl wore a blue anorak. I don't remember what the guy in the glasses wore. I remember the leather jacket because the guy in the glasses kept calling him Hard Core while the girl kept calling him Brian. I remember the girl well because she had such large teeth, such a large mouth, and when she spoke it seemed to me like a huge monster gobbling up calm. Hard Core said something to me. I told him I spoke English. So he said, Fucking cold, right? I must have been shivering. I didn't say anything back. I didn't think I was supposed to. But it pissed him off. He said, mumbling, turning back to his friends, Asshole. I guess that was why his buddy called him Hard Core. The guy in the glasses said, Fuck that guy, Hard Core, forget it. You're right, said Hard Core, then he laughed—a flustered laugh—and said, Whatever, try to be fucking nice. It was hard to say nothing, but easy to see how irrelevant responding would be, how pointless it would be to have an argument out here, or simply skip to reconciliation, go straight to the bit where he buys me a beer, says I'm the coolest guy he's ever met, and reveals that he is the opposite of hard core, he is just afraid and young.

I finished my cigarette and tossed it beyond the barrier. I didn't feel like drinking my beer anymore, so I put it on the ground and left it there, and went looking for the bathroom. You had to walk back to the front, go down a staircase of wet and mildewed concrete, into a little maze of corridors. I found the men's room and had to stand in line for the urinal, which was just a trough filled with ice. I saw Zaid ahead of me in the line, reading the screen on his phone. Someone behind me recognized him, and yelled his name. He turned around and saw me, and for a moment looked as though he thought I was the one who had called out to him. Then he saw his friend. I looked back and the friend was pointing at me. They spoke. At that point, everyone in the line turned around and looked at me. I said nothing, did nothing. I only thought that this night, the eve of a life that I hoped would represent the entombment of the violence I have witnessed or imposed upon the world, seemed headed for violence. I pictured myself picked up, thrown in a urinal full of ice, and beaten by everyone in the bathroom. I thought of Hard Core coming in after it was done, finding me half alive, and urinating on me. I remember thinking, Oh well, because I did not really care. But as soon as everyone had turned to have a look at me, they turned back, and it was over. Zaid went back to his phone, and pretty soon it was his turn at the urinal, and a little later it was my turn.

And then I found myself back at the pool table, where Saskia and Manuela and the man with the mustache still had not finished. It had become something of a spectacle, and a large crowd was standing around the table. The guy was so drunk, Saskia explained when I made my way to her through the circle that had formed around the table, that they kept having to explain which balls were his, and that he had to hit the white ball first. Manuela said, We're going to win. I watched them for a little while. They didn't hold the cue correctly, or stand correctly, or eye any angles, or hit with touch, or understand a single physical concept about the game that could have helped them. I thought that was pretty damn funny. So did everybody else. The guy with the mustache kept telling them he was about to start taking the game seriously. Saskia missed a shot — everyone cheered loudly, because it was an easy, easy shot, and she had missed badly — and came to stand beside me. Why are we so bad? she asked. Who cares? I said. Yeah, except I'm not having fun anymore. When it was Saskia's turn again, I stood beside her and talked her through it. The guy with the mustache objected. He wagged his finger. What did he say? I asked. Saskia did not know. I told her to point to where the ball needed to be hit, then aim to hit it there with the cue ball. Okay, she said. Now, I said, bend your knees, and hold the cue as flat to the table as possible. Like this? she said. Don't grip the cue, I said, just let it rest there. She released her index finger. Just like that, I said. She hit it. She potted it. The whole place groaned. But Saskia was happy. She said, That was easy! Manuela high-fived her and tried to high-five me, but I said, I don't high-five, and shook her hand. The guy with the mustache, whom everyone had stopped paying attention to, must have felt we'd broken some rule, because he shouted something, and when we looked we saw he had the cue ball in his hand, and he threw it at us. I don't know which one of us he'd hoped to hit, but he hit Manuela, in the back, between the shoulder blades. And Manuela dropped.

But that isn't right. It's not what happened. I push the sheets off me. I've set the heat too high. My mouth is dry. I've had six weeks of uninterrupted sleep, and now I am awake and I'm not even tired. Each thought I have gets up on its own legs, grows arms, grips me, lifts me higher and higher into an awakened state, and marches me toward the morning, which is still hours away. I sit up, finally, turn the light on, and see the glass of water I set on the nightstand. I reach for it and drink it. It's lukewarm. I get up and go to the thermostat, which is in the hallway. I turn on the light, and by the door are my boots, still wet, salt-stained, and dripping water on the floor. Above my boots my new coat hangs on a hook, and on the hook beside it I have hung my new scarf. I turn the light off, go into the kitchen, flick on a small lamp, pour myself another glass of water, boil the kettle, wait while it boils, standing in my T-shirt, pajama bottoms, and bare feet, drinking my glass of water and refilling it and drinking it and refilling it and drinking it. When the kettle is boiled I make some green tea. I let it sit while I go to the bathroom. I wash my hands and face and go back to the kitchen, crack the front window open to let cold air in, and smoke a cigarette at the kitchen table. And there, alone, in the subdued and satiny lamplight, I think, again, That did not happen. It had not happened. The man with the mustache had not thrown the cue ball. After Saskia potted her shot, and I shook hands with Manuela, the man simply quit without paying his debt, placed his stick against the wall, and drifted away, and the rest of the evening—at least the hour or so longer that Saskia and I spent there—passed strangely but without incident. How, I ask myself, had I remembered it as though it were real? How had my mind, even briefly, believed in it? I sit back down at the kitchen table and light another cigarette and let the false memory play out. It is corrupted now, but it still contains sensation: Manuela, hit between the shoulder blades, drops. She bunches her back up. Saskia bends down to help her. Janos and Zaid throw themselves on top of the man with the mustache, then more friends come along. They really give it to the guy. Saskia shouts at them to stop, not because she cares about the guy with the mustache, but because nobody is paying attention to Manuela, and she is badly hurt. She has gone pale. A group of people come inside from the smoking area, having heard the commotion, and more people from the front area, and I realize then that there is going to be a great and unfortunate misunderstanding that is going to get a lot of people injured. Nobody who has arrived late knows why the guy on the ground is being pummeled, so they begin to pull people off him, who resist, and the fight spreads backward. I kneel down over Manuela, with Saskia. Saskia says, What do we do? Just hold on to her, I say. I'll go get the manager. When I stand, I see that Hard Core is back, trying to calm everybody down. I try to pass but he steps in front of me. I say, Please get out of my way. He doesn't move. He is frightened by all this violence, but it has thickened in him. His blood has stopped flowing. I say, Well, go ahead, Brian, and he swings at me. He is four or five inches shorter than me, and he does not know how to punch. He misses and I push him down to the ground, not angrily, without heat; I simply place him there, and he realizes he shouldn't get up. And that is where the story ends. But that is insufficient. I pour myself another cup of green tea and watch the steam rise out of the cup. I blow on it. And the scene rewinds. It goes back again. There he is again, Hard Core, in front of me, just before he is about to throw his punch, and I grab his open mouth with my hands, pull it open, and I break his jaw by physically unhinging it from his skull, just pulling — I have his head in my chest, and pull his face open until it pops. I leave him on the floor.

I stand up, feeling an uneasiness that goes everywhere in me, down to my toes and fingertips, into my lungs and eyes, and makes me dizzy. I need to walk around. I open the cabinets. I find a mostly full bag of flour. There are also some jars of spices. I open a few and smell them. Cumin. Paprika. Caraway. I open the refrigerator. Nothing is there, except some lard. The lard has been opened — one of those greaseproof paper wrappers that butter comes in. I take it out and set it on the counter. I see a bite mark on it, or maybe it's a fork mark. I lean in. It looks like teeth to me. I go back to my room. It's about four in the morning. I still don't feel tired. I have a few books. I could turn on the radio. I don't have a TV. What I really want to do is go to sleep. I'd like to sleep until the sun comes up. I open the door to the living room and, even with the curtains closed, I see that the room is bright. I walk to the windows and pull the curtains back, and I see something unexpected and wondrous. The clouds have come way down, and the streetlamps are glowing violet. The violet light smashes upward, then reflects off the heavy, low clouds upon the snowy graveyard, and rises up pink. It is a wild, breathtaking sight. It makes me think of the way I imagine the outer boundary of the universe to be, not black, not vast, not raging, not full of electric storms or combusting debris, but cloudy, bright, and snowing little pink particles of dust. There is nobody walking around, obviously, though it would be nice and mysterious to see a man or woman standing on the sidewalk, or wandering around the headstones. I

stand at the window for a little while. It might be five minutes or it might be ten minutes. I remember that I have
not hung the painting Saskia and I bought together. It's
leaning beside the couch. I look around the room at the
various paintings and prints that came with the apartment, all bland, and decide to remove one that features a
snowy landscape. I take it off and place it on the floor. I
take the painting Saskia and I bought and hang it there.
I step away from it. It seems level. Then I go back to the
kitchen and close the window, because the apartment is
finally getting cool again, and I grab the little radio in the
kitchen, take it to the living room, plug it in to a socket,
and raise the antenna. I scroll through the bandwidth. It's
an old radio, so it has a dial. I don't know what I'm looking for. I start at the bottom, at 88. There is a lot of odd
music in this city. I go very slowly. The squelch between
the stations is nice, that sizzling and scratching you ride
right into the sweet spot—I did some work for Peace 106
in Baghdad, and I remember lots of afternoons when I sat
in my hotel, holding a little silver Sony single-speaker FM
radio, which ran on batteries, rolling the dial from 106
to 105 and back to 106 and on to 107, and back again,
very slowly. Here, in my apartment, I go all the way up,
and find what sounds like a weather report. It is, so far
as I can tell, just names and numbers, cities and tem-
peratures, delivered without inflection. I sit down on the
couch and imagine the man who is reading these. I pic-

ture him in a bright room under long fluorescent bulbs, wearing a white shirt and a navy-blue tie, undone. Every few minutes he pauses. I presume this is when he flips a page or has a drink of water. Or he might be on a loop, and this is a bulletin he recorded an hour ago, which will play every hour until six a.m., and in that case I am thinking of him driving home, wearing a huge puffy brown jacket with a furry hood, and large square spectacles, and he drives as languidly as he speaks. If somebody cuts him off, he brakes, checks his rearview mirror for oncoming danger, and speeds up again when it is clear. He drives so slowly that people overtake him on dangerous stretches of road, simply because they believe his car is malfunctioning. Curiously, he has never, not even once, turned the dial on his radio to himself, to hear himself speaking. He is in his late forties. He is the kind of guy who takes apart his remote control, draws a schematic, then rebuilds a remote that is ten times the size, full of huge buttons, which only he can use. He drinks milk that is five or six days past its use-by date, because he believes the whole idea of use-by dates is an industry conspiracy. He reads fantasy books that are written for children. He washes the leaves on his plants with a damp cloth. He does not like other people, yet he lurks in their radios at night, a voice from beyond, outside geography and time and temperature, as if he might, by the power of his own disintegrated life, save them.

During my second stint in Baghdad, about two weeks after I'd had that cryptic conversation with the inspector at the police station, and about two weeks before I left for good, I was getting a lift from Forward Operating Base Rustamiyah back to the Green Zone, rolling down Route Pluto at about fifteen miles an hour in a convoy of Humvees, when we stopped abruptly because somebody at the front of the convoy had become concerned about a water buffalo standing by the side of the road. This was in eastern Baghdad, in the spring of 2007, and IED attacks were on the rise. Insurgents placed them in trash, in dirt, and in—or sometimes under or behind—dead animals. This one was, however, alive—bleating, stomping, and swatting flies off itself with its tail. I would be told, later that day, that the man who raised the alarm, a PFC named Schaefer, did so because he saw the animal chained to the fence, but by the time the story had got passed down, vehicle by vehicle, along the convoy, the story was that somebody had spotted a wire coming out of the animal's ass. I was, that day, shitting it, since I knew I'd be leaving soon. When your days in a dangerous place are numbered, as mine were, your response to danger changes. My mind had already begun its departure. I spent a great deal of time in those last few weeks in daydreams, corkscrewing out of Baghdad International, rising up over that vast brown swamp of smoke and trash, higher and higher, until the moment we were free, out of rocket range, and the sky was beautiful because it was so dry and blue, and the desert was beautiful because it was so old, so important, and endless. We waited there a long time. We watched for movement all around us. On one side of the road there were empty fields, dotted with trees, and on the other were clusters of habitable, gray, boxlike structures—though they were a good distance away, perhaps a thousand yards. Another PFC named Gomez slowly made his way to the water buffalo. Gomez had received a morals waiver. The Army had loosened its recruitment standards, which meant people could join up despite a criminal history—mainly serious misdemeanors but also felonies like aggravated assault, burglary, robbery, and vehicular homicide. The only things that seemed to absolutely rule you out, as far as your criminal history went, were multiple felonies or heinous sexual crimes. But the reason I remember Gomez was because, as we waited for him to reach the animal and confirm the sight of wires coming out of it—or whatever it was that he was ordered to do—I had a sudden desire to take his place. The weather was weirdly cool and cloudy, and there was an orange-pink light coming from a gap between the horizon and a stack of clouds that filled the rest of the sky. Gomez jumped the fence and walked around the animal, very carefully. He moved slowly. He knelt down. He stood on his tiptoes. He cleared bits of brush all around the animal with his rifle. When he seemed to be satisfied that it was not a threat, or,

I suppose, that it was not being used to conceal a threat, the tension in his body evaporated. His shoulders loosened up, his stride got casual, and he started to jog back toward us. Somebody shouted a question at him as he was running, and he shook his head and twirled a forefinger in the air, and everyone started jumping back into their Humvees and our engines started up again, and we were off, again, at about fifteen miles an hour, heading back to the Green Zone. As we passed the animal and cleared what, I suspected, would have been the blast zone, I felt great relief that nothing had happened, that Gomez had not been killed, that there was no IED, no ambush, and so on, and the man sitting beside me said, All good? and I gave him a very sincere thumbs-up, but very soon after that, and before we returned to the Green Zone, I realized that everything contemptible in me was contained in that sense of relief, or, maybe, in the gesture that expressed that relief.

Saskia and I left Chambinsky before one, to catch the last trains. The place stayed open until six a.m., but I wasn't drinking anymore, and I began to sense that everybody thought of me as a bit of tedium. When it was proposed that I play pool, I was evasive and said I was no good. I said good-bye to Manuela. I said good-bye to Janos and Zaid and then broadly to everyone. They were just settling in. Saskia said she didn't want to stay with them. She was tired, and she wanted to have the breakfast we had planned, and we could not have that breakfast hung over. We needed appetites. We needed to be rested. I agreed. We walked down a long avenue of closed stores and empty benches. The temperature had dipped sharply, and my hands were starting to freeze inside my gloves; maybe I was just getting too tired to feel warm. She was chatting about types of cheese that go well with breakfast. She mentioned smoked salmon. Do you like hot chocolate? she asked. Not really, I said, but let's have some anyway. There were large red globes strung high above the avenue, which descended toward a large, brightly lit square, where we would separate. How many courses are we up to? I asked. Saskia started to count, on her fingers, the number of courses she'd planned in her head. I stopped at a crowded late-night stand to buy a bottle of water for myself and an orange soda for Saskia. There was a long wait, because the people in front of us couldn't make up their minds. It was a couple in their sixties — a man with silver hair and a thin black coat, who wore neither gloves nor hat, and a woman in a thick fur coat, wearing very high heels. The woman couldn't decide whether to get a slice of pizza with pepperoni on it, or one with spinach. You know, said Saskia, there really is no limit to the kinds of food you can eat for breakfast.

ABOUT THE AUTHOR

Greg Baxter was born and raised in Texas. During the past twenty years, he has lived variously in Ireland, England, Austria, Chicago, Louisiana, and Germany. In 2010 he published his first book, the critically acclaimed *A Preparation for Death.* He now lives in Berlin, where he writes and translates.

The Apartment

A Novel

by
Greg Baxter

DISCUSSION QUESTIONS

Please note that these questions and the author interview contain spoilers about the story.

1. We never learn the name of the narrator, nor the city in which he is living. What role does this anonymity play? Have you ever wanted to be anonymous?

2. At one point, the narrator says, "A friend once told me that the only time you ever really see a place is the first time and last time you're there — the day you move in and the day you move out." Is it true that we remember only the exceptions and that the experience of daily life holds little significance?

3. THE APARTMENT has no chapter divisions. What role do chapters have in reading for you? What is the impact of reading this way?

4. The events of THE APARTMENT occur over the course of a single day; however, memories, regrets,

experiences, and recollections of the narrator, as well as stories from the lives of other characters, punctuate the novel throughout. This structure is reminiscent of Virginia Woolf's masterpieces *To the Lighthouse* and *Mrs. Dalloway*. How do these memories serve to add significance to the story at hand?

5. The narrator of the book is in some ways very deliberate in his actions and words, and in other ways completely resigned to the will of those around him. What, do you believe, accounts for this discrepancy? What aspects of your life must you control, and what parts do you leave up to others?

6. Throughout the novel, there are a handful of factual digressions into topics that interest the narrator — the evolution of perspective in painting, an investigation into the Chaconne. In many ways, this feels accurate to the ways in which we often absorb information. What is the significance of these passages and how does this information inform the novel?

7. The narrator has experienced the war in Iraq in two roles: as a member of the navy and as a private contractor, giving him the means to travel to Europe but also saddling him with darker memories. What does this compromise tell us about the character of America as a nation?

8. Saskia is many things to the narrator: companion, tour guide, real estate agent, and translator. Upon

meeting him, Saskia began to define the narrator's life in many ways. What does this tell us about happenstance as a significant force in our lives?

9. The dynamic between the narrator and Saskia seems to be straddling the line between a friendship and a romantic relationship. What is the difference between intimacy and romance? Is there real romance building between these two characters? If so, why don't they choose to indulge in it?

10. THE APARTMENT has a subtly complex ending—one character departs, and another is awake hours later in the middle of the night, listening to the radio. What meaning does this jump in time have in a novel that has, for the most part, taken place in real time?

11. THE APARTMENT is quintessentially the story of an American abroad. What does it mean to be an American abroad—and what does it mean specifically for the narrator—if America is, to some extent, an empire in decline?

12. Have you ever lived abroad? If so, how did that experience shape your concept of America and of yourself?

A TALK WITH GREG BAXTER

THE APARTMENT takes place in an unnamed European city, and we do not ever learn the narrator's name in the book. Why did you decide to leave these two facts unknown, particularly since there is rich detail throughout the novel?

An "unnamed" city wasn't quite my intention. A more accurate word to describe the city is "unreal." This city does not exist (neither does the desert city in which the narrator grows up). There are parts of this place that correspond to my memories of cities such as Vienna, Budapest, Paris, Riga, Stockholm, Berlin, and on and on. But none of the details in the book strive for factual accuracy, and, beyond these warped and untrue impressions of cities I've gathered over the years, the rest is simply made up. I suppose I spend so much time on details because the less real a place is in fiction, the more the reader needs to see it and sense it to experience it. Making the city unreal also allowed me to balance its calm beauty with a sense of hallucination or nightmare.

I've always liked the idea of unnamed narrators. In a practical sense, the narrator didn't start the book with a name, and I never found a suitable moment to introduce it. In a more spiritual sense, he never wanted one.

The search for a place to live is such a universal experience. What makes a specific place a home, and what is the narrator's relationship to the idea of home?

I'm less consciously concerned with the idea of home and more concerned with alienation. The things that might define home for this narrator — his memories, his nature — torment him. What he seeks is separation, an irreversible detachment from all the things that we associate with "at-homeness."

Yet I must admit that I created this fictional city in order to give my imagination a place to live. As I wrote the book, I was living in a drab and characterless suburb in north Dublin (I can get a Dubliner to wince just by naming the suburb). I felt stupefied, numbed, and frustrated. Writing about a man seeking alienation in an unfathomable city was, possibly, a way in which I could study my own definition of home.

My father was born in Vienna. He and my grandmother left Vienna after World War II — my father was three — and he grew up in Texas. It was impressed upon me from an early age, by my grandmother, that we were all displaced Viennese. Perhaps it was meant harmlessly. I took it seriously, and I've visited so often that Vienna has attained an "at-homeness" that equals or rivals what I think of when I think of where I grew up. And Vienna is one of the inspirations for the city in THE APARTMENT.

Why did you choose to set the action during the Christmas season?

December in central Europe is about as far as my imagination can travel from the desert the narrator comes from, and the extreme contrast between environments felt important.

Although the heavy snow might have been more credible in January or February, the desolation of these months — which, of course, await the narrator — seemed too much like the desolation of the desert. In January and February, you can't find anybody on the streets. The cafés and bars are empty. The cold is unbearable. But in December, everything is crowded, and the cold is wonderful. I wanted the narrator to feel intoxicated by the cold and by the city's old and wise vitality.

The violence of the novel is not shown. It is implied, or perhaps not real. Why did you choose to keep it off-stage?

One of the consequences of showing a violent event in the narrator's past is the introduction or suggestion of psychological motivation. I'm suspicious of novelists who think of themselves as psychologists, and I really loathe and mistrust motivation as a principle in literature. In THE APARTMENT, a man searches for an apartment in an unfamiliar, foreign city. The story takes place on a single day, and during that day he remembers things that have happened to him, and things he has done. If something violent were introduced, something significant and traumatic in his past, it would have instantly become the central motivating engine of his psychology—his propulsive psychological appetite. If there had been something in his childhood, something violent, the whole novel would have become about the relationship between childhood trauma and adulthood. If I'd shown something violent in Iraq, it might have turned this book into a story about post-traumatic stress disorder. So keeping the violence offstage, so to speak, was a way to maintain natural complexity and avoid psychological oversimplification.

I also wanted to write a book in which the intensity arose not from the fulfillment of the need to witness violence in order to purge or understand it, but to suppress it in order to make it inescapable. For me, this process begins and ends with language, or how the narrator chooses to phrase his thoughts. The central struggle of this book—for me as author, anyway—was the narrator's wish to resist his nature and his past through a commitment to plain, simple observations of the present.

You are an American born in Texas but have lived abroad for almost two decades. Why did you leave, and how has living outside of the United States influenced the themes and ideas that you wrote about in THE APARTMENT?

THE APARTMENT might very well be an attempt at an extended answer to these questions. The book actually came out of the ashes of a failed essay on why I left the United States, and how living abroad had changed me. The questions were too complex for an essay. Everything I wanted to say felt untrue.

But THE APARTMENT wasn't influenced as much by living abroad as I was influenced, as a writer, by the literary influences I've embraced over the last decade. I now read a disproportionately massive amount of fiction in translation—European fiction, especially. At times I feel like I am studying my own alienation from a literature I should have inherited. And to me it's increasingly obvious that the city in THE APARTMENT, among many other things, is—or was in 2010—my vision of the European novel.

Within the tight narrative structure of THE APARTMENT, there are many digressions, flashbacks, and stories. What roles do these anecdotes play? How did you choose what stories to tell about the characters?

I wanted to try to have the narrator hold on, as intensely as possible, to the present tense, and let him fail to do so only when the strain became too great. The book began partly as an experiment in how far present-tense, moment-by-moment narration could stretch. I didn't get very far. The narrator starts to interpret his observations, his interpretations link to memories, and those memories require interpretations, and these interpretations link back to the city. This method of interchange—the spontaneous and unexpected connections the narrator makes—made the subject matter curiously secondary to the way in which subject matter is encountered. The book ends up, I hope, feeling a little bit like a mystery constantly unraveling.

Secondary characters such as Manuela, Josephina, and Janos come across as being as complex as Saskia

and the narrator. In such a short novel, how were you able to create such memorable and real characters?

Well, I don't know how memorable or real any of my characters are, but I try not to know my characters. I assume that everyone, in real life, is both complex and perfectly ordinary. The more I spend time with people, the more depth our relationship has. But ultimately, if I respect somebody, I must accept that they are unknowable. I try to carry that approach into fiction. I don't create characters with personalities. Rather, I observe the behavior of characters. If an author resists the temptation to type his or her characters, those characters will usually contradict themselves and become vital. If the characters act consistently, they're useless or they're props. No character should fill space, and no character should have a defined role before they appear in a book—they should not serve a purpose. Janos could have been more or less important. Manuela, too. They turned out how they turned out. Importantly, I think, a character is only worth putting in a novel if they are—or could be—worthy of being the main character of another novel. No character should ever be, by nature, minor.

Why did you set the narrative to take place during one day and why did you not include chapter breaks?

For a long time, I struggled with the question of how to structure novels. I finally realized that the concept of structure was entirely alien to the way my mind conceived of stories. I wanted to write something small and quiet—something profoundly simple in its conception but that could achieve a level of complexity, suspense, and purpose through details, subtlety, and suppressed intensity. But everything I began collapsed the moment I began to consider the book as a question of structure. This book is the result of having finally learned to let structure arise spontaneously.

Is THE APARTMENT an allegory?

No, definitely not. But I suspect, or hope, that it looks like one. I found myself creating a book so conspicuously repetitive, in terms of imagery, phrasing, places, and action, that it seemed almost preposterous to suggest that the book was *not* allegorical. But these images, places, and acts have no relation to external concepts—they only have a relation to each other within the text, and they transform the book, I hope, into a perpetual contradiction machine.

Is the romance present in THE APARTMENT really there, or is it an expectation the reader brings to the book?

It was not my intent to subtly convey a blossoming and inevitable love affair — which would have cheapened the book profoundly. Nor was it my intent to define or limit their relationship in any way. The narrator and Saskia certainly like each other. They're polite to each other. And there's something about his search that draws them together. From the narrator's point of view, however, his relationship to Saskia is the first major failure on the path to separation. It gives him a sense of hope and direction and possibility. These things, for him, are illusions. Yet he persists in this mistake, maybe because it diminishes the pain of his journey. Or maybe because he genuinely likes Saskia. Or because he feels Saskia might genuinely like him. Or a hundred other reasons. In the end, in his new apartment, we see him confront the pointlessness of his desire to separate himself, as well as the pointlessness of trying to alleviate the pain of separation. But it's also impossible for him to go back. His memories — even his most recent memories of the night out with Saskia — enter into a cycle of despair that, each time it begins again, casts off another layer of safety and illusion.

Do you consider THE APARTMENT an anti-war novel?

I don't. At least I think I don't. War takes up such an infinitesimal proportion of this book, and I don't want readers to feel that I have tried to express something true about the nature of war, or have tried to boil down the narrator's fundamental despair as being somehow a consequence of his war experience.

And yet there is, in the book, a contemplation of the relationship between intervention and injustice — something more modest than a protest, something less certain than a political position. Positions themselves are acts of violence in America, at least the way I remember things. The narrator of THE APARTMENT is not aloof or unmoved by suffering, but he sees injustice and suffering as inevitable consequences of intervention, or of having entrenched opinions.

ABOUT TWELVE

TWELVE

TWELVE was established in August 2005 with the objective of publishing no more than twelve books each year. We strive to publish the singular book, by authors who have a unique perspective and compelling authority. Works that explain our culture; that illuminate, inspire, provoke, and entertain. We seek to establish communities of conversation surrounding our books. Talented authors deserve attention not only from publishers, but from readers as well. To sell the book is only the beginning of our mission. To build avid audiences of readers who are enriched by these works—that is our ultimate purpose.

For more information about forthcoming TWELVE books, please go to www.twelvebooks.com.